BLADE & BASTARD
—Warm ash, Dusky dungeon—

Kumo Kagyu

Illustrations by so-bin

Words of true
power raced from
Iarumas's lips.

He opened the
spell book inside his head.
HALITO is not going to cut it...
MAHALITO wouldn't either.
LAHALITO might—but there
was no guarantee.

SEZMAR

A FIGHTER WHO LEADS THE
ULTIMATE PARTY.
THIS JOVIAL MAN IS ALSO FRIENDS
WITH IARUMAS.

AINIKKI

AN ELVEN WOMAN OF THE
CLOTH IN THE SERVICE OF GOD.
LOOKS OUT FOR IARUMAS AND
GARBAGE.

GARBAGE

An adventurer rescued by Iarumas. The "monster's leftovers," who speaks more like a dog than a person.

IARUMAS

An amnesiac adventurer. Retrieves the bodies of fallen adventurers from the dungeon at the request of the temple.

RARAJA

Rookie thief. A strange turn of fate leads him to exploring the dungeon with Iarumas and the others.

CONTENTS

BLADE & BASTARD -Warm ash, Dusky dungeon-

TABLE OF CONTENTS

BLADE & BASTARD

—Warm ash, Dusky dungeon—

BLADE & BASTARD

—Warm ash, Dusky dungeon—

Kumo Kagyu
Illustrations by so-bin

1

jnc

New York

Author: **Kumo Kagyu**

Illustrator: **so-bin**

Translated by Sean McCann

Edited by C. D. Leeson

BLADE & BASTARD: Warm ash, Dusky dungeon

© Kumo Kagyu, so-bin 2022
© 2022 Drecom Co., Ltd.
First published in Japan in 2022 by Drecom Co., Ltd.
Wizardry™ is a trademark of Drecom Co., Ltd.
This English edition is published by arrangement with Drecom Co.Ltd.,
Tokyo in care of Tuttle-Mori Agency, Inc., Tokyo.

English translation © 2022 by J-Novel Club LLC

Yen Press
150 West 30th Street, 19th Floor
New York, NY 10001

Visit us at yenpress.com
facebook.com/yenpress
twitter.com/yenpress
yenpress.tumblr.com
instagram.com/yenpress

First JNC Hardcover Edition: December 2023

JNC is an imprint of Yen Press, LLC.
The JNC name and logo are trademarks of J-Novel Club LLC.

The publisher is not responsible for websites (or their content) that are not owned by the publisher.

Library of Congress Cataloging-in-Publication Data is available

ISBN: 978-1-9753-8975-8 (hardcover)

1 3 5 7 9 10 8 6 4 2

LBK

Printed in the United States of America

BLADE&BASTARD

—Warm ash, Dusky dungeon—

Prologue
All-Stars

"Mimui woarif! (*Let there be light!*)"

And in the darkness, there was light.

The dungeon, hazy in the faint glow, echoed with a single footstep.

No, there is never just one footstep.

Instead, a crowd of footsteps. Six people moving, each at their own gait, each clad in their own mix of gear, with no consistent uniform. Even so, they never broke formation.

These were adventurers.

"Hey, Sarah, can't you use a better spell than that?"

The stone stairs stretched onward. A man, irritated by their length, spoke in a voice that sounded like a groan. In the pale-green light, he appeared to be a fighter outfitted in a full coat of mail. As he kept bellyaching, his large helm, which bore an ornamental statuette of a crouching dragon, swayed heavily from side to side.

"MILWA fades in no time," he griped.

"What, you want me to cast LOMILWA? I refuse, Sezmar."

The one who answered him was a delicate, beautiful young girl. She wore a breastplate on top of her priest's robes and had a look of composure on her face. Her long ears—reminiscent of bamboo leaves, and a good match for her charming face and lithe body—swayed as she spoke.

"But if you're fine with me not being able to identify the monsters with LATUMAPIC, or protect you with BAMATU, then I wouldn't mind casting something stronger."

Sezmar started to say something, gave up, then tried to speak again before ultimately falling into a sullen silence.

Upon seeing their leader (who always led the charge into battle) reduced to this mood, one diminutive adventurer in leather armor smiled to himself. Because of his short stature, he could've been mistaken for a child, but the smirk on his face was that of a grown man.

"You mighty humans sure do have it tough, huh?" the man remarked. "Not being able to see in the dark like we can."

"If you can't say anything nice, don't say anything at all, Moradin. Neither a rhea like you nor a dwarf like me can see through the darkness in this dungeon."

The one chiding Moradin was a bearded man who shared his companion's short stature. His face, however, was twice as wide, and his muscular body was built like a rock. This man wore a horned helm, carried a war hammer, and spoke in a voice that was every bit as solemn as you would expect from his appearance.

"Whoops. I know that, of course, High Priest Tuck," said Moradin.

"And you, Sarah." High Priest Tuck turned his attention to her. "When you chastise someone for their behavior, you should speak a little more gently."

"Okayyy…"

Under normal circumstances, an elf would never readily accept the criticism of a dwarf. However, Sarah was still a mere priest, whereas High Priest Tuck had finished his training and become a mighty bishop. Sarah knew she had no hope of winning if she talked back to him, and she was highly averse to arguing anyway.

It'd been a long time now since the life spans of the fairy races like elves, dwarves, rheas, and gnomes had shortened to become close to that of humans. Sarah was an elf, but she was still just a slip of a girl—though the beauty of her face was greater than one would expect for her young age, she was no older than she appeared to be.

"We still aren't down to the next level, are we?" Sarah complained. "My feet are killing me."

"You said it," muttered another adventurer.

This man was Prospero, a mage who was just as frail as the young priest. The length of these stairs had taken a physical toll on him as well. He put some weight on his staff, using it for its more traditional purpose, then took a deep breath, wiped the sweat from his brow, and spoke once more.

"The depth of this dungeon transcends human knowledge."

"It *is* a dungeon, right?" Sarah murmured. "It's not just a cave... It was made by someone."

"It truly is fascinating. Who created it? How...and for what purpose?"

"That's what we're gonna find out," Sezmar replied, unable to take any more of their complaints and speculation. If he let the spellcasters debate, who knew how old he'd be by the time they were done?

"Hawkwind, any sign of the enemy?" asked Sezmar.

"None."

This man, Hawkwind, was dressed like some sort of spy, and his nature as a man of few words supported that image. However, his five fellow travelers knew that he could be surprisingly droll and pleasant too.

Hawkwind seemed to savor the experience as he said what was on everyone's mind. "Finally, a new level..."

Sezmar, Sarah, Moradin, High Priest Tuck, Prospero, and Hawkwind.

The faces of these six adventurers were tense, but also full of irrepressible excitement. They were standing on the very front lines of clearing this dungeon. This was a new level—no one had ever set foot here, and it had never before been visited by others. There would be dangers, yes, and threats, no doubt. One of their comrades might lose their life.

But who cares about that?!

That's what Sezmar had said when they'd decided to unlock the sealed staircase.

This staircase had been behind a massive door. Each of these types of doors blocked off the next level of the dungeon, and they were present on every floor...at least, so far. Were they meant to ward off intruders, or to keep something in? Until that door—which had a frightening number of sigils and unfamiliar letters carved into its surface—opened, there was no advancing to the next level.

Here, on this day, at this time, they had located this level's door, and Sezmar's party would be the ones to open it. What was an adventurer if they were afraid to venture forward? Unknown riches might await. The glory of taking that first step would undoubtedly make them the talk of the town. And, information on an unexplored level was worth a fortune all on its own. They didn't have a single reason not to proceed.

Clank! The sound of Sezmar's own iron boot against the stone floor made him tense up.

"What're you all spooked for?" teased Sarah.

"Sh-Shut up…!" Sezmar stammered, shooting back at Sarah for her somewhat shrill comment. Moradin failed to completely stifle a laugh and took a breath beneath his iron helmet.

This was new territory for them. It was important for Sezmar to stay on his toes, but getting too worked up wasn't good either.

"Okay, let's do this," declared Sezmar, taking a determined first step forward.

Silence.

"Hm? What's wrong?" Sarah asked.

Their leader had frozen up, almost as if petrified. Sarah leaned forward to get a glimpse of his face (despite the iron helmet!), but Sezmar didn't say so much as a word. Was it a trap? Or an attack from an unknown monster? If he was paralyzed, was it time to use the DIALKO spell she'd been saving?

"Dariarif…" Sarah whispered, speaking the first word of the spell without meaning to.

A moment passed, and then…

"Hey…" Sezmar muttered in a strained voice. This time, it was Sarah's turn to jump a little.

"What is it, Sezmar?" Moradin asked cautiously, his voice low. Hawkwind had already fallen into a defensive posture.

Having come this far, the adventurers were ready to engage in combat with unknown threats at any time.

"We're...the first adventurers...to have reached this level, right?" asked Sezmar.

"What are you talking about? Of course we are." High Priest Tuck spoke in an encouraging tone, trying to assuage whatever fear Sezmar was dealing with. "The great door was sealed, and no one had opened it. You know that better than anyone, surely."

Sezmar continued without responding to High Priest Tuck. "Prospero...the door really was sealed, right?"

"Yes." Prospero nodded, ready to turn his staff toward any threat. "That should be correct."

"Sezmar..." Sarah groaned. "What's the matter? Are you really spooked?"

"Well, then..." Ignoring Sarah's teasing—an attempt to distract from her own fear—Sezmar gestured with his chin. The elf's eyes followed his line of sight, darting to where his iron helmet was facing, to a space beyond the area lit by her faint magical light.

Shoulders quivering, unable to stop himself from laughing, Sezmar finally said, *"Who're all these dead guys...?"*

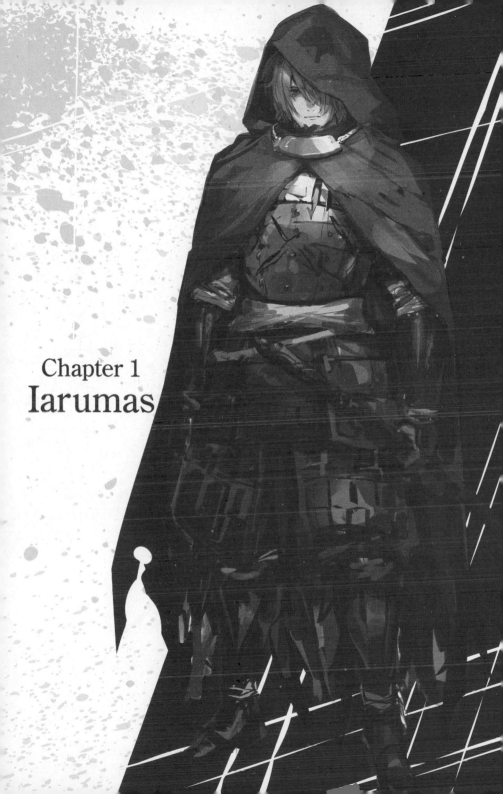

Chapter 1
Iarumas

Whoosh! The scent of ashes swirled through the air.

Murmur turned to prayer, prayer to incantation, and then, to command.

Pray.

That word was not for the living. It was for the one who'd once been here, the one yet to be lost.

But what was he to pray for, exactly?

Hopes. Wishes. Attachment. Resentment. Duty. Obligation. Obsession. Desire.

Why do we live, and why do we die?

Those things are not known to the living. Nor even to the dead. Why would death bring enlightenment about the things we couldn't understand in life?

And yet, in the silence, sometimes an answer is spoken. A voiceless cry. A wordless appeal. A scream, squeezed out from the soul.

But there are those for whom even that is not possible.

Their voices make no sound. Their words remain unformed. They haven't even the strength to cry out.

Is it resignation? Acceptance? Or simple exhaustion?

Whatever it is, this young adventurer who'd fallen—

"Rodan...! You've gotta be kidding me?!"

—had turned to ash.

As they stood before the mound of ash crumbling on the altar, his companions, who had been looking on, cried out in anguish.

It was a scene that seemed out of place in the quiet temple, but was a daily occurrence here, even a horribly familiar one to Iarumas. He stood, back to the wall, arms crossed, watching as the adventurers grieved.

He'd seen this scene before, more times than he could remember. That was why Iarumas felt nothing as he strode forward with a powerful step, almost as if he were kicking off from the stone floor. Under his dark cloak, a black-lacquered stick made a rattling sound.

The black rod.

The adventurers noticed Iarumas not because he was there, but because of that sound.

"It's too bad."

Iarumas's words were sincere—it *was* a shame. But, this Rodan fellow's luck had run out. He felt that from the bottom of his heart.

Eight eyes turned toward Iarumas as the four people gave him piercing stares. The harshness of it seemed to remind him of something he'd been forgetting, so he added, "About both of them."

Parties traditionally consisted of six members. He didn't know how it was elsewhere, but that was how Iarumas saw it, and how the people of this town did too. Yet, the number of adventurers in this stonework shrine—once you excluded Iarumas—was four.

It was unfortunate, rotten luck. Failing to resurrect two of their companions. There was no more to it than that.

"Now, as far as payment goes," continued Iarumas, "the two I brought back here were carrying equipment and money—I'll be taking half of it."

"You're going to talk about money *now*?!"

Iarumas felt that he had only stated the obvious, but one of the adventurers apparently felt otherwise. The brawny fighter grabbed Iarumas by the front of his clothes, squeezing as he tried to lift his slim body into the air.

It wasn't causing Iarumas much damage, but he didn't like the way it made breathing difficult.

"There's no need to make such a fuss," Iarumas said with

exasperation, his voice hoarse. "They just turned to ash." It wasn't as though their souls had been lost. As far as he was concerned, he was speaking the unvarnished truth, even if it was no comfort to these people.

"You ass!!!"

But it seemed that his words hadn't reached the fighter, who proceeded to take a swing at him. Iarumas absently traced the path of the man's fist with his eyes, angling his head a little to the side, and...

"Stop that at once!"

The fist froze as a dignified voice echoed through the shrine. It wasn't magic, but those words did have power behind them. The voice belonged to a woman. A young girl. One whose habit couldn't hide her feminine beauty. Two long, thin ears poked through the silver hair that spilled out from beneath her wimple.

This was Aine—Sister Ainikki, an elf.

This girl, who worked as a servant of God in the temple, looked at each of the adventurers. "Isn't death a sign that they lived a good life and were allowed to enter the City of God?"

Seeing the fighter's face turn from red to blue, Iarumas thought she'd just poured fuel on the fire.

"You saying it's *okay* that they died, then?! Huh?!"

"We must live well and die well," said Aine. "That's common sense, isn't it? No one can change that."

"He turned to ash! No...you people incinerated him! You botched the resurrection!!!"

"We did not fail!" Aine's voice sounded hurt, but her tone wasn't going to be persuasive. The fighter set down the scrawny priest and turned his fangs on the girl instead.

"Then why did they—?!"

"God is saying that they lived the best lives they could, and there is no need for them to come back!"

It was a good thing. Even now, as the fighter glared at Aine with a face twisted in rage, she believed in her words from the bottom of her heart. Her proud smile, peaceful and without a hint of malice, made even these dungeon-hardened adventurers hesitate for a moment.

Having taken this as a sign that they wanted to hear her preach the teachings, Aine's eyes narrowed happily. "Of course, we are allowed to delay death...if, by living on, the deceased would be of greater value. Should you wish to resurrect the two of them, we must demonstrate the possibility that your companions will do even greater good. Otherwise, God won't be convinced."

In short, she was saying that this party needed to make a larger tithe. This would show God that, if the two adventurers were still alive, they could be of even greater value to the world. The higher price for their resurrection indicated that God had recognized the worth of these two adventurers' lives. Why could their friends not be happy about that? Aine didn't understand...

"Enough of your pious cant!" the fighter shouted angrily, spittle flying. He then decided to storm out of the temple's shrine, tearing open the door and slamming it hard behind him.

Iarumas watched absently as Aine declared "Well, now!" with ears and eyebrows raised. He hadn't really planned on intervening if the fighter decided to clobber the girl, nor would there have been any need for him to. But he was glad that the disturbance was over—he didn't want to waste more time than necessary.

"Sorry 'bout that, Iarumas."

Iarumas looked at the face of the dwarf who'd spoken to him. A fighter, of course. He was a member of the other fighter's party.

This dwarf and Iarumas were acquaintances, having seen each other at the tavern occasionally, but they hadn't talked much. Iarumas didn't remember the dwarf's name either. He only knew the name "Rodan" because the other fighter had shouted it, so he'd assumed it to be the fallen adventurer's name. The only important details about a person were their level, class, and in the case of spellcasters, what spells they knew. That's why Iarumas fell quiet for a moment, not sure how to address the dwarf.

Regardless, it seemed that whatever sentiment the dwarf had inferred from Iarumas's silence was positive, because he started making excuses. "Our leader just lost two of his companions, so he's agitated right now...not thinking clearly."

"It's fine. I'm not bothered." It was true. None of this fazed Iarumas.

The frontline fighter had survived, while the mage Rodan, and one other—the party's priest, perhaps—had died. They'd likely suffered a flanking attack that had messed up their formation, causing their back row to be killed. The party had then run off in the confusion, leaving their fallen companions behind. They'd had to ask Iarumas to retrieve the bodies, and then the resurrection had failed. The loss of members and money was going to make it hard for their party to recover—their exploration would be delayed considerably.

"I don't blame him for losing his cool. But...progress has been slow for everyone lately," said Iarumas. There was no need for the party to rush. They weren't going to fall behind the others seeking to clear the dungeon.

Iarumas offered some words of condolence. The dwarf got very quiet. So, Iarumas continued: "Could...I ask you to pay me now?" This was important. But, at the same time, not absolutely vital. "If you can't, it just means I won't retrieve any of you the next time I find you. Nothing more."

"Well, that would be a problem for us," the stout dwarf said, wincing. He produced a bag of gold coins. "If you happen upon us down there, bring us back, would you?"

"Got it. If I find you, I will." Iarumas took the gold without hesitating and stuffed it inside his cloak. The weighty coins felt so reliable. They could do a lot for him, after all.

"So long, then," said the dwarf.

"Yeah." Iarumas nodded. "Tell him not to let things get him down too much."

The dwarf, who was leaving with the rest of his party, didn't give any response to Iarumas. Instead, the door opened much more quietly than the last time, footsteps passed through it, and then it closed again.

Iarumas was left alone with Ainikki in the stonework shrine. With the faint scent of ashes hanging in the air, a despondent Aine murmured, "Why do you suppose he got so angry...?"

"Because the resurrection failed."

"It did not fail!" Aine's hair danced in the air as she quickly turned her beautiful eyes toward Iarumas. "That's their misunderstanding. God thought those people had lived valuable lives, so there was no need for them to do things over!"

When she acted so indignant, Aine looked awfully immature, which was a sharp contrast to her elven race.

No—in this era, Iarumas had heard that even elves and dwarves didn't live any longer than humans. As magic faded from the world, fairies had also come to be not so different from other people. These days, the other races were just a little faster, a little more pretty, or a little more sturdy than humans. And trivial differences like those meant nothing to Iarumas. He knew that, as they delved into the dungeon, those differences would eventually disappear.

"But more importantly!" Aine's lyre-like voice shot up an octave. "I haven't forgotten! You haven't been able to show God your value yet, Iarumas-sama!"

"I'm grateful for my resurrection," Iarumas droned in a disinterested tone, stating his honest feelings. "But I don't believe I bear the responsibility for it."

"It's that bad attitude of yours that keeps God from recognizing your life as having greater value." Aine put her hands on her hips, thrusting out her chest as if trying to emphasize the lines of her body beneath her habit. "As such, you must show God that you can live a better life!"

"So, you're saying 'go collect more corpses,' right?"

He didn't particularly mind.

Iarumas spent his day-to-day hauling the remains of adventurers—people he didn't even know—back to the surface. It was only natural that he be allowed to take their money and equipment for doing so. After all, they wouldn't be getting any use out of them if they were never revived. Sometimes, as was the case today, he was even hired to retrieve bodies by other adventurers. Again, he didn't particularly mind doing it, or mind paying the tithe to the temple for their resurrection.

But...

"I'm an adventurer. Not a retriever," Iarumas declared, as if confirming that fact with himself. He took a relaxed breath, then exhaled the same words he did every day, his breath unwavering: "Has anyone I might know been brought in?"

"No, sadly." Sister Ainikki gave him the usual response in the same timbre as every other time. "Honestly, I don't think you should get your hopes up…"

"I have to keep going until I find my companions. I can't move on." With that said, Iarumas headed for the door out of the shrine.

Behind him, he heard Aine tell him to take care and then start murmuring the words of a prayer. He gratefully accepted this, opening the door and crossing the threshold before closing it behind him.

What kind of sound did it make? He wondered about that, but it wasn't worth dwelling on.

Once he left the temple, the blue sky and blanching sunlight assaulted Iarumas's senses. He began to walk, squinting in irritation at the pain in the back of his eyes, which had grown accustomed to darkness.

He was on a suffocatingly narrow cobblestone road in the middle of the city, which had just about everything crammed onto it. The street wasn't unique in that regard. This fortress city had tried to stuff all the things the world had to offer inside its walls, so every street was like this. They'd gathered up everything in an attempt to keep a lid on what frightened them—that was to be expected.

The only exception to this was a place on the outside of town—a big hole.

"Hey, look at that."

"Iarumas, huh…"

"Iarumas of the Black Rod…"

"He's a corpse looter."

"Damn that maggot…"

"I hear he got resurrected by mistake."

"Lucky bastard."

"Who even knows how true his story is? What kind of man doesn't remember the things that happened in his past?"

As Iarumas walked toward that place, he heard passersby on the street—other adventurers—grumbling.

It didn't matter. He didn't think their opinions had any bearing on him advancing deeper into the dungeon.

Suddenly, Iarumas thought he detected the scent of ash on the breeze, which made him smile. It was a pleasant smell, and an awfully familiar one, like that of wet streets after the rain.

§

In ancient times, long ago, the people forgot it.

Who can say how many years passed after that? One day, when no one knew it had ever existed, it abruptly returned.

The dungeon.

This magical hole, suddenly gouged out of the land, was literally overflowing with power. It plunged deep into the ground—no one knew how far—and was filled to the brim with monsters and treasure.

Naturally, many self-proclaimed heroes, saints, and sages braved its depths one after another. Many of the evil villains who roam our world also attempted to seize the dungeon for themselves. All of them were swallowed up by it, destroyed.

A descendant of the legendary hero. A great sage who spent their life in the study of magic. A brash youngster from the village.

Inside the dungeon, they were all equal—the weakest of the weak.

No one knew what the dungeon was. They only knew two things, and perhaps, just one.

Treasures lay sleeping within, ones that transcended the imagination. The dungeon was also home to man-eating monsters and filled with lethal traps.

In short, all anyone knew was that the dungeon was a place beyond the comprehension of mankind—a completely different world.

People came to view the dungeon as dangerous, so they kept a respectful distance from it. But the products that came from the dungeon were—in a variety of ways, and to a variety of people—still alluring. There was no shortage of people who ventured into the dungeon seeking wealth and fame, to do deeds of arms, or for some other purpose.

Dying repeatedly, overcoming danger, and seizing treasure—some gradually adapted to the dungeon.

In time, people came to call them…adventurers.

§

This was the first underground level of the old, moldy dungeon that'd once been forgotten by all. Many adventurers now came and went from this place, and Iarumas didn't mind setting foot here.

It was customary to descend into the dungeon with a party of six, but, no, he didn't mind doing it alone.

"Now then…"

Iarumas looked around—the stones comprising the dungeon had been laid so neatly that it was unnatural. This scenery of unremarkable stonework continued on endlessly—or so he was told. All Iarumas saw was darkness, and white lines stretching out infinitely.

The grid of the dungeon.

Just how much distance did one segment represent? Iarumas didn't know. No one did.

Some claimed it was only a few steps; others said a city block. Still others alleged that the distance could span across an entire town.

Inside the dungeon, you couldn't trust your senses, including your sense of time or distance. That's why Iarumas chose to think of the segments this way:

One space on the map.

No more, no less.

Iarumas was used to this place. He knew where to walk and how. But he pulled a bundle of graphing paper out of his cloak anyway and began flipping through it, as was his usual habit.

"What level should I go down to today? That's the question."

It should go without saying, but delving into the dungeon solo was an act of insanity. But, well…that's *if you were trying to clear it.*

Iarumas carefully advanced toward a door that someone had already kicked in. When he stepped into the burial chamber that lay beyond it, a faint smell of blood hung in the air. There were corpses here, yes. But not of adventurers—they were the chopped-up remains of monsters.

"An orc, huh?"

These humanoid corpses belonged to fiends with ugly, piglike faces. Two or three orcs lay in pieces next to an open treasure chest. Many of their wounds looked far from fatal, so the battle must have been long and drawn out.

"Rookies, then."

Having concluded this with one glance, Iarumas stepped over the orcish remains without any great concern.

Orcs were among the weakest creatures in the dungeon. Although, obviously, it was actually *people* who were at the very bottom of the dungeon's ecosystem. In that sense, orcs were still a terrible threat. If a party couldn't defeat them, they would get nowhere fast down here.

These adventurers hadn't lost anyone, or at least, hadn't left their friends' corpses behind and fled, so they had some potential.

"Hm…?" Iarumas crouched down to examine the corpse of an orc he had been in the middle of stepping over.

The killing blow is different…

It was precise. And sharp. Unlike the other wounds, this one had clearly been dealt by a veteran.

Well, that's not so unusual, I guess? A more experienced adventurer was leading rookies through the dungeon. Nothing surprising about that.

Iarumas examined the wound for a moment. Once he was satisfied, he continued walking at a relaxed pace. Not to a closed door, of course. He headed to a burial chamber—the door here showed signs of having been kicked in.

Corridors and burial chambers. Monsters that guarded them. Sleeping treasure.

These things were infinite, yet at the same time, limited.

That might have seemed paradoxical, but it was the truth. There *was* an end to the dungeon. Also, it wasn't as if an unlimited amount of monsters and treasures would appear. Once someone killed the monsters and took their loot, they wouldn't show up again for a while.

Another rule of the dungeon: each burial chamber had just one group of monsters. This meant that, if you followed a path someone else had already cleared, the dungeon would be safe.

Safe, huh?

Iarumas smiled at the thought. Maybe it would be more accurate to say that the path would be *comparatively* safe.

Some monsters roamed. There were traps. And, most importantly, by following an already cleared route, you were giving up on any treasure chests or chances to do deeds of arms.

That was the cost of a little safety—something which was rare in the dungeon—but it was an absurd thing to do.

Roaming in the darkness of the dungeon like this, Iarumas was seeking just one thing:

The corpses of adventurers.

After continuing for a while, Iarumas stopped a few spaces ahead of a crossroads and held his breath. He pressed his body against the wall, lowered his hips, and slowly, slowly leaned forward.

Iarumas could already hear them. Footsteps. Metallic sounds. Several of them. Approaching.

"GORROOGG..."

"GROOWL..."

Around the corner came wet snouts. Doglike jaws. These were armored kobolds.

The three kobolds were grumbling about something as they marched around the dungeon.

Are they coming this way? Iarumas clutched his weapon under his coat, glaring into the darkness. He called up a map of the dungeon in his mind, found a nearby burial chamber he could flee into, and routed out how to get there. Failing that, if he was forced into a battle...what spot would be most advantageous for him?

By the time all this information had flashed through his brain, the footsteps of the kobolds were already fading away.

Iarumas breathed a sigh of relief.

Is it time?

This was a baseless instinct—a gut feeling, the product of

experience. If you came across roaming monsters, that was a sign of something happening in the dungeon.

Iarumas took a tool from his pocket—an ancient golden coin with a string tied around it—and threw it down the corridor. The coin bounced off the floor, rolled, fell over, and then…nothing. He reeled it in, and then advanced one space.

Iarumas called this tool the Creeping Coin.

Monsters, traps—spinning floors and pitfalls—and unknown items that had been discarded by other adventurers… These were the threats he used the Creeping Coin to probe for. Monsters would pick up the coin, and it could trigger floor traps in Iarumas's place.

It was also lighter and easier than swinging a stick.

This coin which bounced along the floor was Iarumas's only companion during his exploration.

So, well, he wasn't that lonely.

§

No corpses, huh?

Iarumas clicked his tongue. The sound echoed a little inside the dungeon.

It wasn't the lack of corpses that irritated him. No, it was that *corpses* were all he could think about. Iarumas had gone through a number of burial chambers after encountering the kobolds, following the trail left by those who'd come before him.

And what did he have to show for it? Nothing.

There were no corpses, and therefore, nothing for him to retrieve. All he'd found were the remains of monsters.

"Kafaref nuun darui (*Follow the spirits of the lifeless ones*), huh?" He spoke the words of a spell, KANDI, which he couldn't use—obviously, it didn't do anything. Iarumas would have to look around by himself.

He didn't mind the effort. It was always like this. Not a problem.

Still, it upset Iarumas that he'd been so fixated on the lack of corpses. Delving into the dungeon, walking around all day with nothing to show for it, pulling out. Then, doing the same thing the next day.

He couldn't let himself resent the process. It was his daily life. The way things ought to be.

I'm thinking like I really am a corpse retriever... It must have been because of what Sister Ainikki had said to him. Iarumas slowly shook his head.

Black scorch marks extended out in front of him.

Yes, scorch marks. The floor of this burial chamber was blackened from being badly burned. Iarumas could sense that, if he touched the floor, it would still be hot.

He also knew that this wasn't magic. This sunburst pattern emanating from the center of the burial chamber was a scar left by an explosion that had filled the room. Flames, a shock wave, and searing wind. Its power had been lethal.

No one used a spell like that on the first level. The monsters here weren't that smart, so if there was a spellcaster who could have done this...

They wouldn't have fired it off here—they'd have wanted to save it.

It might be a bother dealing with small fry, but no one was going to be foolish enough to throw away a high-level spell on them. Mages always had a limit to how many words of power they could store in their minds. Those who wasted them died fast...and this was a bit deep inside the first level for it to have been a test fire.

That only left one answer.

They got caught in an explosion trap, huh?

Probably. Iarumas always had to add that qualifying word. They *probably* messed up opening a treasure chest.

Was it the thief's blunder? Maybe this party's thief had been paralyzed before getting to this point, but they'd forced themself to try and open it anyway? There weren't any monsters that inflicted poison or paralysis on this level, but there were needle traps of both types. If the thief, who was tasked with opening treasure boxes, had gotten hit by one of those, then it would've been a common rookie mistake to keep going.

Calling it a mistake might not be fair.

Everyone wants to make up for their losses. Go a little farther, take a little more risk—if we do these things, we can get it all back.

23

That was the kind of place this dungeon was. If someone was going to venture here, they knew going in that it was somewhat dangerous.

Still, calculated risk or not, the result was the same—the bomb had gone off, and they'd been hurt bad. Since there were no corpses here, the party hadn't been wiped out. They must have pulled out without abandoning the bodies.

Either that, or…they'd kept exploring.

Surely not.

If that adventurer with the sharp sword skills was with them, they'd never do such a thing.

Iarumas left the burial chamber, uncharacteristically immersed in thought. He mechanically threw the Creeping Coin, which he was holding in one hand, onto the floor ahead. It bounced along the hall making a little clinking noise, and then…

BEEP! BEEP! BEEP! BEEP!!!

Iarumas started, snapping to attention, then instantly lowered his hips and braced himself. He looked around in all four directions.

The thing causing this cacophony was one of the dungeon's traps—an alarm that called for monsters. He didn't know if the monsters served some kind of master, but the effect was the same either way. Once an adventurer triggered it, they had two options: fight or flight. Not that they had any chance of getting away.

They're not in this burial chamber. But Iarumas was clearheaded and could sense them… On the other side of multiple walls.

He rapidly reeled in the coin, then pressed his ear against one wall of the burial chamber. This chamber was part of the route the monsters would travel, and he didn't want them nabbing him as an extra prize on their way through.

The clatter of armor. Shouting. Screams. Monstrous howling. The morons were…

This way?

Iarumas crawled through the dungeon with shadowlike caution. As he slipped through one open burial chamber, then another, he noticed it right away.

Blood.

The stench of burned meat and boiled blood. It could only mean one thing…

They set off that bomb, but recklessly tried to press onward anyway, only to trigger an alarm?

"Idiots," Iarumas murmured without emotion. They'd brought a skilled fighter with them and had still made a mess of things.

When he reached the fourth burial chamber, Iarumas finally found what he was looking for.

"OINK! OINK!!!"

"WHINNY…!"

Humanoid creatures—three, no, four orcs, holding weapons and squealing excitedly. These monsters looked like pigs standing on their hind legs, and were among the weakest creatures in the dungeon. They were still stronger than humans, though. Just like pigs were.

The corpses now lying at the orcs' feet were exactly what Iarumas had been searching for.

This party had already been exhausted after the explosion and fighting, and then…the orcs had gotten reinforcements. After being surrounded and battered with axes and clubs, the party members were very clearly dead. Their corpses each carried their own equipment, burned but only slightly damaged. In total, he counted…five bodies.

Five?

At this point, Iarumas realized that something was wrong.

"Woof!" From inside the pile of corpses, there came a high-pitched bark, like that of a little dog.

Peering closer, Iarumas saw a small, thin adventurer—filthy and dressed in rags. The leather armor under his cloak was rotting, and he wielded only a simple longsword. Iarumas thought he looked like a young boy—no, a stray dog with greasy, curly hair.

The stray's neck bore a rugged collar that was probably worth more than all his other equipment combined.

There was a chain—not a particularly long one—binding that collar to the wrist of one of the dead.

"Growl!!!"

That's why the adventurer couldn't move around very well. He was just holding his sword and barking.

Get any closer and I'll slash you...or bite, he seemed to be saying.

But no one fears a chained beast.

Although, maybe these pig-brained orcs lacked that kind of intelligence.

"OINK! OINK!!!"

They surrounded the chained fighter on four sides, pointing and laughing at him mockingly with crude snorts. It was like they were saying, *We've got a real lively one for dinner tonight, boys!*

The fighter pulled his chain along behind him, swinging his sword around despite the restraints. The sword flashed through the dungeon's miasma, sharp and fast. But it was too lacking in spirit.

His blade grazed one orc's snout, making the beast falter, eyes wide with surprise. That was all.

"WHINNY!"

The orcs were quick to mock their friend for being intimidated by the surviving adventurer. It didn't like that. Winding back with its club, the orc grunted as if to say, *Watch this.*

What would happen next was obvious—there'd be another body added to the orc's kill list.

Five, six, it made little difference. So...

"Hea lai tazanme (*Flames, come forth*)," Iarumas whispered. He tossed the flame that formed at his fingertips into the void. The dark red fire burst with a cracking sound, engulfing the chain that tethered the adventurer and melting it in an instant.

Outside the dungeon, this technique would have been considered something special, but here, it was just called HALITO.

"WHINNY?!"

"OINK?!"

The pig-heads panicked. The fighter's eyes—clear and blue—pierced Iarumas.

"Do as you please."

"Arf!" With only a bark in response, the stray dog went rabid and lunged, sinking his teeth into the throat of his prey.

The other pigs screamed, and a splatter of blood vanished into the darkness of the dungeon. When the orc went down, drowning in its own blood, its head was only barely still attached to its body.

Having accomplished this with a single blow, the fighter pounced on his next victim. The way that he plunged straight forward, sword in front of him, wasn't so advanced you could call it swordsmanship.

But it was fast, sharp, and lethal.

"OOOIIII—?!?!"

"SQUEEEE?!?!?!!!"

Death cries from a second orc, then a third.

In the time it took the stray to attack, the last lucky orc survivor figured out that all its friends were dead.

"OINK! OINK!!!"

Faced with a hopeless situation, the orc elected to flee. Squealing, with tears and snot running down its face, it fell over itself running away on all fours like its ancestors.

As the monster passed Iarumas, he stepped aside to make way. It didn't even look at him as it disappeared into the deep darkness.

"Woof...!" the doglike adventurer barked reproachfully at Iarumas.

"There's nothing to be gained by killing it now."

The adventurer seemed confused, either about the orc, about Iarumas, or about himself. Since the adventurer just kept staring at him from beneath his cloak, Iarumas held both hands up where they were clearly visible.

He didn't know if his meaning came across, but as he approached, the adventurer just looked at him in silence.

That was convenient for Iarumas.

He started stuffing the corpses—which were only a few steps removed from mincemeat—into the sacks he'd brought with him. He did the same with their equipment and other stuff. If he brought it all back, it'd be worth money, so he could handle a little extra weight.

It's what adventurers do.

While he was working, Iarumas came across the chain that had tethered the doglike adventurer. It had turned a yellowish brown when it melted. He gave it a sniff, then kicked it away.

He figured these adventurers were the kind of guys who would take advantage of youngsters who'd just arrived in town. They'd help themselves to their victim's worldly possessions behind the tavern, then, if the victim was lucky—or unlucky, perhaps—they'd use him as a meat shield. And because they'd left all the fighting to their meat shield, they'd gotten no experience for it, and had ended up like this.

Is anyone going to want to resurrect these guys?

The temple didn't discriminate, though. If Iarumas brought them in, the temple would hold on to the bodies, and Aine would be grateful.

The adventurer was glancing in Iarumas's direction, so he looked right back.

"If you plan on resurrecting them, bring the money to the temple."

"Grrrowl…?"

It didn't matter to Iarumas if the adventurer understood what he said or not.

Gritting his teeth against the weight of the ropes digging into his shoulders, Iarumas started dragging off the bodies.

That's why, even when he heard the patter of steps behind him, he didn't really pay them any mind.

§

"Hey, Mifune! Isn't that Garbage?"

Iarumas, who had been stirring a gray, mud-like gruel, absently looked up when he heard that voice.

It was a knight—a fighter, not a lord—who was carrying a dragon helmet under his arm. This masculine man with blond hair and blue eyes looked out of place in every way you could imagine. After all, Durga's Tavern was a hangout for adventurers—it wasn't anywhere a knight should be.

For one thing, the title of knight meant nothing here. The armies and chivalric orders that different countries kept on throwing at the dungeon only ended up getting swallowed by its depths. Not many were eccentric enough to go on calling themselves knights after that pathetic showing, but this man, Sezmar, was one of those rare free knights.

Iarumas gave Sezmar a dubious look and let the spoon in his hand fall into the bowl of gruel.

"Stop it with that nickname."

"Oops," said Sezmar. "Forgot you didn't like Mifune... Sorry, sorry! You mind if I sit down and eat with you?"

"If you're not afraid of corpses, go right ahead."

"Nothing scary about corpses...s'long as they're dead."

"I suppose you're right."

Considering that he'd been eating right next to a pile of body bags, Iarumas wasn't one to cast aspersions about it. Besides, Iarumas had never really been all that concerned about Sezmar's background. He knew the man was a good-aligned fighter, and that he'd reached a high level. That was enough.

Sezmar sat down at the round table and started ordering. "Hey, get me some ale and meat! Fried boar leg! And potatoes!"

"Where are the All-Stars?" Iarumas asked, picking his spoon back up.

"We're all off on our own, doing whatever we like." Sezmar grinned, setting his helmet down on the table. He then pointed to the other side of it with his chiseled chin.

"More importantly, man... You're partied up with Garbage now?"

"Arf?"

That bark came from the ragamuffin adventurer seated across from Iarumas and Sezmar. The way he buried his face in the bowl of gruel as he ate was rather doglike. He'd taken his hood off now, and his mess of curly hair reminded Iarumas of a little puppy as well.

"He, uh, seems to have tagged along with me. Just keeps on staring, even when I'm eating, so I fed him," Iarumas explained, breaking off a hard piece of black bread and dipping it into his gruel. Then, taking what was left of the bread, he looked across the table at—

"Garbage...?"

"Woof!"

—and tossed it to him.

"What, you don't know?" Sezmar asked. "Well, I guess you've never really cared much about any other living adventurer either."

"You're biased." With a look at Garbage, who was chewing the newly acquired bread, Iarumas took a bite of his own.

Sezmar let out an exasperated sigh. "Normally, that's not the kind of name you give a person."

"Oh, yeah?" said Iarumas. "It sounds like a fine name to me."

It's more than one syllable, at least, Iarumas thought.

Sezmar didn't respond immediately, but instead, silently tore into the roasted meat that the waitress had brought. After wiping the grease from his fingers, he said, "Well, there's a story behind it. Want to hear?"

"If you feel like telling it."

"Sure, I'll tell you all about it."

From what he'd heard—and Sezmar emphasized that this was *just* what he'd heard—Garbage meant just what it sounded like.

The other day, a slaver's cart had been attacked near the town. Well, nothing was unusual about that. Ever since the dungeon had appeared, monsters that'd been largely forgotten had gradually started to return. They'd torn into the slaver's "cargo," feasting on it. It'd been a hellish scene, bodies everywhere, and...

"This kid was the only one left. He didn't get eaten."

"Yelp! Yelp!" exclaimed Garbage.

Did he not realize the two men were talking about him? Or was he just not interested?

Garbage was too busy gobbling up his unappetizing gruel. Under the specks of food now attached to it, his crude collar shone with a dull luster.

"So anyway, he's a slave," explained Sezmar. "He doesn't speak, and he acts like a dog. The guys who found him—"

"They tried to use him since he was disposable, but somehow, he was the one to survive, right?" Iarumas finished.

"Exactly. And that's why I know his name."

"So not even monsters will eat him," murmured Iarumas. "He's left-overs... Garbage, huh?"

He should've ended up dead a long time ago, but he'd survived. Most famous adventurers were that way.

He's lucky. That's one thing you can say for him, thought Iarumas. He'd at least done better than getting robbed out behind the tavern and then beaten to death.

Sezmar downed his ale with a hearty swig, then wiped his mouth with the back of his fist. "Here I was, thinking you'd bought him, Iarumas."

"I'm not enough of a villain to go buying and selling people."

"Then you could've just saved him."

"I'm not that good of a person either."

"So you're standing in the middle. Neutral, huh?"

"That's right." Iarumas nodded, then gave Sezmar the rundown of the day's events. There was nothing to hide, but nothing to boast about either. Just another day.

"Hmmm," Sezmar murmured, taking a sip of ale. He looked at Garbage. The kid's curls bounced around as he munched away. "Well, it's not easy, maintaining that neutral balance. Is it your way of training?"

"When it comes to killing techniques, they say it helps to have just the right amount of evil in you. But maybe I just don't think about these things all that deeply." Iarumas spouted off some nonsense, scooped the last bite of gruel into his mouth, and put down his spoon. When Iarumas stood, the movement of his chair made Garbage's head suddenly shoot up.

"Watch out," Sezmar quietly warned as he chewed his roasted meat down to the bone.

Iarumas cocked his head to the side and asked, "For what?"

"The kid's party may've been wiped out, but that doesn't mean their clan's been destroyed."

Clan. Iarumas smiled at the unfamiliar word. He'd heard that adventurers had been forming clans recently. He knew it just meant a group of adventurers, but it still sounded ridiculous to him.

Better than a guild at least.

Laughing, Iarumas replied, "He's been following me around on his own, so it's not like there's anything I can do about it."

Garbage hopped down from his seat and started using his rags to wipe the gruel off his face. Iarumas watched him do that, then, in a murmur, added, "It's not my problem."

"He doesn't think it's a problem either."

"You've got a point there." Satisfied with this, Iarumas took hold of the rope that was binding the body bags together and gave it a pull, hoisting them up. Their weight bit into his shoulder, and he felt a little hesitant about going up to the second floor of the inn.

Seeing this, Sezmar got a smirk on his face. "Oh, come on. Are you gonna sleep next to those corpses?"

"Nothing scary about them as long as they're dead, right?"

"Damn straight."

Iarumas started walking. The corpses trailed behind him, dragging noisily along the ground.

"Arf!" There was also a little bark, and the sound of light footsteps.

"But you know..." muttered Sezmar. "Now that I get a fresh look at him, I could've sworn I've seen that face somewhere before..."

Because of the noise, Iarumas didn't particularly notice that final murmured comment.

§

As Iarumas opened the door to the room he was renting, Garbage slipped inside.

"Hey..." he called out after the kid.

Garbage responded with a questioning whine and then curled up in the corner of the room, just like a dog or cat would. He was even expressionless as he did it, acting like it was perfectly natural behavior. When Iarumas called after him, Garbage just looked up as if to say, *Do you need something?*

It was a small room, but better than sleeping outside. One bed, two adventurers, and a bunch of corpses. Easy math.

Iarumas kicked the bodies into the room, then strode over to stand wordlessly next to Garbage.

"Yap?! Yap?!"

With a blank expression, Iarumas picked up the little ragamuffin by the scruff of the neck. The kid started yelping. Ignoring his doglike protests, Iarumas threw Garbage's surprisingly light body onto the bed.

"Aruff?!"

"If you're going to sleep, then sleep there. This is my spot."

"Woof…?" Garbage regarded him with suspicious eyes. Iarumas snorted, then sat down in the corner of the room. When he began using one of the corpses as a pillow, Garbage let out a small, "Arf."

"Don't let it bother you. Just go to sleep already."

Iarumas seemed indifferent, so Garbage eventually gave up and curled into a ball on top of the blankets.

It's like sleeping in the stables.

Iarumas found this arrangement to be more comfortable than a bed. When he slept in a bed, it made him feel like he was getting old. If he ever found himself *wanting* to sleep in a bed, then it was time to pack it in and quit being an adventurer. The cold hard floor, the time he spent with corpses—it was all just a part of his day-to-day life.

As he drifted off, Iarumas thought, *I'm sure I always did this in my past life too.*

He dreamed of the scent of ashes. Familiar…that's how it felt.

§

The next day…

It was perfectly natural to keep your distance from a man dragging corpses through the street in broad daylight. It was an unnerving sight, even if he *was* on his way back from the dungeon…and perhaps, even if it hadn't been Iarumas doing the dragging.

Iarumas didn't seem bothered by any of this—he walked along in silence. To him, corpses were corpses, and as long as they didn't start moving on him (either through resurrection or by becoming undead), then he was fine. If someone were to press Iarumas for an opinion on them, he might reply that they could be a handy place to store items occasionally, but that was about it.

Once out of the inn, Iarumas didn't stop walking. There was just one thing that differed from his usual routine…

"Arf!"

A little shadow trotted along behind him.

The presence of some monster's leftovers—Garbage—did nothing to affect people's impression of Iarumas. The creepy guy now had a filthy adventurer tagging along with him. It wasn't a big deal.

Dragging, trotting, whispering. Dragging, trotting, whispering.

It was an instrumental duet of dragging corpses and doglike footsteps, with the whispers of bystanders as accompaniment.

This performance ended when they arrived at a fork in the road. Iarumas looked behind him and met Garbage's eyes, which were sunken deep inside the kid's cloak.

"Yap?" Garbage tilted his head to the side.

Iarumas let out a deep sigh. "I'm doing this anyway," he murmured to no one in particular. "The more corpses the better, I guess…"

Without further deliberation, he turned down a side street. This path didn't lead to the temple—it went to the dungeon.

Taking corpses to the dungeon? That seemed backward. Bizarre. It made no sense.

"Tch, it's Iarumas. He's creepy."

"A mage, on his own, carrying bodies to the dungeon…? Oh… Is he handing them over?"

"*I wish he'd just resurrect them and be done with it…*" This comment, at least, was something that no one in the city would ever think.

It was all too common for adventurers who didn't want to pay the temple's tithe to cast resurrection magic on their party members while inside the dungeon. In these cases, the adventurers were either too short on cash to pay for resurrection, or at such a high level that they didn't need to go to the temple.

Perhaps Iarumas was headed to the dungeon for a meeting he couldn't hold in public, one with adventurers of a different alignment. Whatever it was, there was a great difference in the success rate of resurrection in the silence of the temple versus resurrection within the dungeon. If you were going to pay someone with the skills a cut rate to do it down there… Well, who knew what the chances of coming back were?

Money, friends, time… It was up to adventurers to decide what they wanted to prioritize. That's why no one thought anything of Iarumas hauling corpses to the dungeon.

Nobody. Not a single person.

§

Iarumas chucked the body bags down to the first underground level, then jumped on top of them without hesitation.

As Iarumas landed with a dull thud—

"Arf."

—Garbage touched down next to him quietly…aside from the bark.

Taking note that Garbage was standing on the stone floor of the dungeon, Iarumas simply said, "Nice trick."

"Ruff!"

The kid was proud of himself.

Iarumas snorted in response, then began dragging the corpses. Not down the corridor, no—to the corner of the burial chamber that served as the entrance to the first basement.

As Iarumas leaned against the wall, arms crossed, Garbage walked over to stand in front of him. The kid let out a whine, cocking his head to the side quizzically.

Iarumas averted his eyes. "You don't have to be part of this, you know?"

"Arf."

"Oh, yeah?"

It wasn't that they'd managed to communicate. After Garbage barked, Iarumas just decided to leave him alone.

Not long after…

"Grrrrfff!!!" Garbage emitted a low growl from deep in his throat.

A shadow passed over the shaft leading to the surface. Several people dropped down one after another.

"Hmm…" They weren't familiar to Iarumas, but he knew their type—a band of six, each with their own diverse equipment.

Adventurers.

"You're late," Iarumas remarked.

Were they, though? He laughed at the utter absurdity of what he'd just said. Time was unreliable in the dungeon. They might've been a minute off. Or an hour. He could have been waiting for a year, or perhaps, a second.

"We're here for what's ours, Iarumas."

A response came from the leader of the party. He looked to be a fighter—Iarumas drew that conclusion based on his equipment and where he was located in his party's formation. Not many fighters stood anywhere but the front row.

The other five adventurers slowly started moving as the fighter—who carried a hastily forged sword and wore mass-produced leather armor—spoke. Iarumas kept track of them out of the corners of his eyes as they fell into battle formation.

On the way to the dungeon, Iarumas had thought he'd sensed someone following him. Sezmar's warning from the other day flashed through his mind.

While Iarumas thought, Garbage emitted a low growl, spittle flying from his mouth.

The leader sized up the two of them. "The kid belongs to us," he declared.

"Don't know what to tell you." Iarumas shrugged. "I don't have a chain for him."

"We're done talking!"

"We *are* done talking." Iarumas smiled. "Though there's no need to say that here in the dungeon." The party was probably after his wallet too. If they weren't friendly, Iarumas had no reason to spare their lives.

The leader began to move, and the moment he pushed the hilt of his sword up with his fingers...

"Howwwwwwl!!!"

Garbage pounced.

The encounter battle had begun.

§

Adventurers were forbidden from unleashing spells or killing one another in the city.

If one of them did go wild in town, it would mean trouble for everyone. Each time an adventurer delved into the dungeon, they edged closer to becoming something inhuman. However, most weren't strong enough to live inside the dungeon just yet.

To that end, adventurers made an effort not to work with those who held beliefs that were different from their own. This was an unwritten rule: every adventurer had an alignment, whether that be good or evil, and this alignment was the most important factor in determining if a group of adventurers could form a party.

If party members carelessly got into an argument or a fight that devolved into swords and spellcraft, who knew what might happen? In most cases, if someone got out of hand, people would gang up and kill them. This wouldn't be a problem for the city guards to solve—their fellow adventurers would do them in.

"Whoops!" Iarumas murmured, reacting swiftly.

"Box them in! There's only two of them!"

An enemy came straight at Iarumas, but he parried their blow with the weapon hidden under his cloak. His boots ground on the stone floor of the burial chamber as he kept his distance, surveying the battlefield.

It was six-on-two. No... *Three-on-one and three-on-one.*

It looked like this fight was more or less going as the enemy had planned it.

"Growl...!"

"Gwagh?!"

"Why, you!"

Garbage's sword flashed, blood flew, and there was a scream...but no one had fallen yet. The party was doing a good job of using its numerical advantage. When Garbage struck at one, the others would rush in from the sides, stopping him.

Unable to take it, Garbage deftly dodged, gradually moving left and right as he bayed like a wild dog.

"Woof!"

Garbage wasn't letting the enemy attack him, but at the same time, he wasn't able to land any of his own strikes. The inability to make things go his way was putting an awful lot of pressure on his animallike mind.

These enemies were no match for him in terms of raw skill, but if he got hasty and it affected his swordsmanship...then there was no telling how things might go.

Guess that means they're better than orcs.

Iarumas revised his estimation of them as rookies. These guys had returned alive from the dungeon two or three times, and that was enough to qualify them as experienced adventurers—in this town, at least.

Knowing how to walk the dungeon made a huge difference.

But Iarumas knew how as well.

"Screw you!"

"Ngh...!"

Iarumas parried their constant attacks, closely surveying the enemy's formation. Only a rookie or an idiot attacked an unfamiliar opponent in the dungeon without thinking it through first.

"Don't give him time to cast a spell!"

"I know that!"

"What's taking them so long over there?!"

Despite their noisy shouting, the enemy managed to keep up coordination, albeit at a bare minimum level. Still, Iarumas skillfully deflected their blades. Sparks flew as weapons collided in the dusky burial chamber, revealing the enemy's faces and equipment.

Any mages?

In the darkness, it was impossible to tell if his opponents were male or female, or what races they were. But those details were immaterial.

Six enemies. Three over there. Three here. No spellcasters here. But what about in the back row? Were any of them holding staves? No. Anyone else wearing light equipment? Yes—a thief with a dagger.

"Die already!"

"All right then..." Iarumas muttered to himself, readying his stance.

Another attack. Iarumas parried repeatedly and then made a big jump backward.

One adventurer already had his sword drawn back for a blow, and when he saw Iarumas move, his eyes went wide. "You're not getting a spell off!" he shouted, seemingly realizing that there was no time to spare.

The fighter at the lead sprang right at Iarumas. "Get dead, mage!"

Instantly, a dry sound echoed through the air.

Iarumas had sunk to a low posture. Blood splashed everywhere. A gout of dark ichor painted the stone walls of the burial chamber.

"I don't recall ever saying I was a mage," Iarumas remarked as the fighter's head *went flying*.

"Whuh…?!"

Murmurs from the man's shocked comrades filled the burial chamber as his decapitated torso slumped to the ground.

Critical hit.

Done in by a single blade. It was in Iarumas's hand, drawn from the black rod that served as its scabbard. The thin weapon was…

"A saber?!"

"Indeed. A *katana*," Iarumas boasted. He'd drawn and struck the fighter in one motion, using only one hand. It was an incredible technique.

But for one who had no desire to understand his words or the reality of the situation, it meant something entirely different.

"Growl!"

The party members had stiffened in surprise—Garbage wasn't one to let the brief moment of opportunity slip by.

The little shadow moved in on them smoothly, his posture low, as if he were running on all fours. The sword he swung was dull. His technique? A total mess. But, he probably did it that way to use his body to its fullest extent. Garbage's sword operated like the fangs of a feral dog, coming in low to tear out their throats.

"Gurgh?!"

"Gyargh?!"

"Agagh…?!"

His sword whistled from right to left. Three times. Three screams. Three corpses.

Inside the dungeon, what adventurers developed was an inhuman level of focus (HP), but not a greater life force.

If you slashed someone, they died. No exceptions.

"Wah, agh, agh, ahh…?!"

Two to go—a fighter standing in front of Iarumas, and the thief behind the fighter holding a dagger.

They had polar opposite reactions; one of defiance, the other of panicked confusion.

"Hi-yahhh!"

It was the fighter who came at Iarumas. Young, straightforward, with bloodshot eyes. Greedy for life. A good fighter.

Iarumas leaned forward.

The swordsmanship used in *this* part of the world was built on a rationale that was completely different from the techniques he knew. This style bludgeoned opponents through their armor, or aimed for gaps in it, seeking a guaranteed lethal blow. Anyone who mocked this technique as a mere resort to brute force would surely die in their first battle.

And so, Iarumas did not.

Instead of committing the folly of meeting his opponent's blade head-on, he shifted himself just outside the fighter's line of attack. Stepping under the sword, he reached for the handle of his katana with an empty hand, brought his fingers alongside it, and then gripped with a sliding motion.

He drew a great arc of silver light.

The flash of his sword, which seemed to graze the stone floor, brilliantly severed the fighter's arms before blasting off into the void. It was a blow made possible by the combined speed and strength of two opponents lunging for one another.

"Gyarghhh?!"

The fighter backed away in terror, blood spurting from the stumps of his lost arms. His eyes were wide with disbelief. He went pale, the blood draining away from his face.

Things might have been different on the surface, but here in the dungeon, this wasn't a fatal injury. It was just a matter of chanting "Darui zanmeseen (*O life, O power*)"—with those words, his wounds would heal and his arms would reattach.

That is, if there were a priest here who knew the spell DIOS.

Even people who would've been treated as the rarest of saints up on the surface only met the most basic requirements for a priest down here. And parties that lacked a priest…met tragic ends.

In the dungeon, the mightiest warrior in the history of the surface was just another fighter. And if this fighter (now writhing in pain after losing his arms) or the others (face down on the ground) could leave the dungeon on their own…

"It would make my job a lot easier."

"Ah—!"

Smiling faintly, Iarumas mercifully stabbed his katana through the fighter's throat, snuffing the life out of him.

That left only one.

"Eek…?!"

He looked like a kid, face full of fear. This young thief had definitely seen all the fighters die before his eyes. He was in a class that demanded quick wits and agility, so maybe he'd even seen it coming before the fighters had.

The kid trembled, quaking pathetically, until finally, he decided on a course of action.

"W-Wahhhhhhhhhh…!"

He fled.

Running, jumping onto the rope ladder up to the surface, and clambering back up it. Greedy for life. Iarumas's eyes narrowed approvingly.

"Woof…!"

"Hold on."

It wasn't approval that made Iarumas hold a hand out in front of Garbage's nose, stopping him from pouncing.

"Yelp!" Garbage peered up and gave him a look of dissatisfaction. The blue eyes hiding deep in his cloak shone like fire.

No, Iarumas's reasoning was simple: "If we wipe them all out, there won't be anyone left to bring money for the resurrection."

Iarumas was half certain he would be seeing that thief kid again.

Leave the dungeon? Run away? He was an adventurer because he *couldn't* leave.

That was the kind of creature an adventurer was.

Besides, this is a good enough haul.

Wiping the blood from his blade on the inside of his elbow, Iarumas returned his katana to its metal scabbard that looked like a black rod. This scabbard matched the black armored leggings hidden under his cloak and blended perfectly with the rest of his eastern-style ensemble.

No matter what happened to anyone in the dungeon, not a soul was going to care all that much. *Who* a person was made little difference—whether it was himself, their enemies, or Garbage. The only ones who did have to care were the priests at the temple who would receive these adventurers' bodies. Sister Ainikki would be delighted, no doubt.

And perhaps, their surviving comrade as well…

Without any hesitation, Iarumas began stuffing the freshly killed adventurers' corpses into body bags. He let out a sigh as he thought about hauling them all back to the surface by himself. Then, he pondered the blue eyes staring up at him.

Letting out another sigh, Iarumas asked, "You want dinner again tonight?"

"Arf!"

Chapter 2
Raraja

The whistling wind sounded like a death knell. Under a leaden sky, the wind died as it slammed against towering walls that grew up out of the wasteland.

Here, there stood a single town. Stone walls—stonework buildings. The town had once been just a village, though its name from back then had long since been forgotten. These days, if you mentioned the dungeon town, everyone understood that you were talking about this place.

Scale—that was the town's name.

It stood as a massive fortress city in the middle of the vast wasteland, surrounded by red earth and thick patches of grass. Scale might have looked almost like a series of grave markers.

But inside, it was different.

The lights never went out, day or night. It was a town that never slept.

This sleepless city was aflush with a startling amount of riches. The bottomless reservoir of dungeon bounty included jewels, gold, magical items... A mountain of treasure. Selling even just one item elsewhere in the world could pay out enough to live on for life.

And so, adventurers gathered—heedless of the risks to their own lives—in order to seek that fortune. They carried the goods that satisfied them back to Scale, flooding it with the dungeon's fortune.

As Scale was filling up with decadence and prosperity, the town's walls were rotting away. After all, no one thought of anything but the dungeon and their own advancement. The once beautiful walls were now little more than mounds of quarried stone. In their current state, they would mean nothing in the face of monsters pouring out of the dungeon.

Besides, if someone were to put a few holes in these walls, they might even be able to secretly carry out some assets to sell…

The area adjacent to where the townsfolk broke down their own walls was the darkest, coldest, most shadowy part of the city.

A single youth trudged along in this darkness.

His face—swollen black and blue. His eyes—constantly watching his surroundings. His body—small and underfed, like a rat.

Occasionally, he heard someone laugh. These were adventurers on the main street, living it up at the tavern, no doubt.

The youth peered in that direction, then clicked his tongue unhappily and squatted down next to the wall. Examining its surface, which was already loose because of all the stones that had been taken out of it, he found the specific stone he was seeking and reached for it.

This stone, which had been shoved in a crevice to look like it fit there, came free with ease. Its role as a cover was now finished. The youth stuck his hand into the hidden hole hesitantly. With just his fingers, he felt around for the object inside, then pulled it out.

What the youth had seized for himself, with a look of desperation on his face, was a dirty little bag. Slowly, he pulled the drawstrings and checked the contents.

One gold coin. That was it.

The youth stared vacantly at the coin. Then, grinning for a moment, he squeezed it.

After replacing the stone in the wall with a kick, he walked off, never looking back.

Even though he had nowhere to go…

§

"Yap?! Yap?!"

Garbage yelped in an unbelievably shrill voice, twisting about as if trying to escape some kind of torture. However, there were frightening opponents in this world, ones that never let their victims escape once captured.

"I know you're an adventurer, but you need to clean yourself a little!"

Foremost among these opponents was Sister Ainikki, with her slender arms, washtub, sponge, and soap.

"Yelp?!?!?!"

"No!" she chastised. "You never know how you're going to die, so you need to make yourself clean while you're still alive!"

Aine and Garbage's battleground was at the back of the temple, inside a washtub filled with water.

Garbage splashed and flopped about in agony, ribs showing on a scrawny frame. The kid was emaciated and acting like a wild dog, but after enough scrubbing...white skin appeared from under all that grime. And, once the oil and grit was washed out, that curly hair would regain the fluffiness it should have always had.

The crude iron collar now looked out of place on the waif's delicate frame.

"Why does this kid have so much blood caked on...?!"

The pure white soap suds that now filled the tub were a testament to Aine's hard work. It had taken changing the water out several times to stop the slurry from looking like dark sewage.

Iarumas, who had been standing by the wall of the temple and watching the proceedings with disinterest, answered her. "The kid wanders off sometimes and comes back looking like that."

"If you're looking after her, then at least take care of her!"

"I'm not, and I don't. The kid just follows me around." Iarumas did his best to explain while letting the devout elf's sermon go in one ear and out the other.

But it seemed this wasn't what the good sister wanted to hear. "Honestly!" she exclaimed.

Garbage shot Iarumas a look that said, *"Don't just stand there and watch! Help me!"*

But since Iarumas had already denied being Garbage's keeper, he felt that he should probably stay out of this.

Hold on...
"Garbage is a girl?"
"God, you're hopeless!"
"Yap?!"

§

When it was all over, the three of them went to the chapel. Garbage was suspended in some sort of a stupor—the girl stared into space like her soul had departed from her body.

In contrast, Aine, who'd made Garbage change into fresh under-wear after she'd finished with the bath, was in a fine mood. She was currently drying the girl's hair with a towel.

Beneath the sunlight that shone into the chapel, the nun looked more beautiful than ever. This was also the first time Iarumas had ever seen Aine smile so broadly.

"You're *that* satisfied?" he muttered.

"Those who live well, die well!" Sister Ainikki declared with a smile.

Is that how it works? Iarumas wondered. Death was death. Nothing more than a result.

But different people came to terms with it in different ways.

If Sister Aine had been able to overcome the inescapable reality that everyone must live alongside, then he could say she was worthy of respect.

"Arf...?!"

"Oh, my."

Garbage suddenly snapped back to her senses, bolting out of the blanket wrapped around her and running away from the long bench.

She—yes, *she*—darted off like a spooked rabbit, growling as she snatched up her usual rags. Aine and Iarumas both watched as she went to cower in a corner of the temple. Aine with a smile, and Iarumas vacantly—that was the only difference.

"So, you were saying that your next exploration will be longer?" Aine asked.

"Well, I don't expect to be back for a few days," Iarumas said, patting the large bag that was sitting next to the long bench.

Though he'd told her it would be a few days, that was measuring by his subjective experience of time inside the dungeon. Iarumas didn't know how long might pass, objectively, on the outside. Regardless, bringing more supplies than he expected to need was a habit for him—he measured the duration of his exploration not by subjective time, but by how much he consumed.

"I'm planning to explore a slightly deeper level."

Why? Because Iarumas was an adventurer. Watching the way he behaved explained a lot.

Aine gave him a half-lidded look of disdain. First, he dragged a girl around looking that filthy…and now, this.

"You're going without any other companions?"

"I might've invited Sezmar if he were around," Iarumas replied.

Yes, *if* he were around. And even if he were, there was no guarantee he would have accepted.

The knight Sezmar's party wasn't at the tavern. They were either on an adventure, or they'd been wiped out. Since no one cared enough to keep track of what other parties were up to, there was no way to know for sure.

Iarumas's only thought on the matter was that, if they had been killed, he wouldn't mind retrieving the bodies.

Sister Ainikki let out a deep sigh. "You don't have any friends, huh?"

"Leave me alone."

That was the end of their conversation.

The temple had no shortage of visitors. As much as they criticized the priests for their hypocritical cant, death and ashes were forever a part of the adventurer lifestyle. Some came in carrying the bodies of fallen companions, while others were wallowing in sorrow. People rejoicing—people raging.

"Sometimes," Aine mused to herself, looking over all the adventurers, "you have to know when to give up." The elf's eyes—which were still beautiful, even if she would live no longer than a human—were focused on Iarumas. "Even if you were able to find the corpse of someone who knows you, it may be meaningless."

"What, is that a warning?" Iarumas smiled faintly. "How rare."

"I am a priest, after all," Sister Ainikki replied, her eyes narrowing. "If you consider how long it took for you to be resurrected, you're *getting on in years*. Don't forget that."

Time ticked away equally for all people, even the dead.

Iarumas shrugged without a word. He didn't even want to think about how old he must be now. As long as he didn't die of old age, it mattered little.

"You flipped a coin, and it happened to come up heads. Maybe it'll come up heads next time too." Aine let out a sigh. Exasperation. Resignation. Concern. It could have been read as any of them. "How many flips in a row will it come up heads, do you think?" she inquired. "And what do you plan to do if one comes up tails?"

"When that time comes," Iarumas replied, "then the next adventurer will take care of it."

Before Sister Ainikki could say any more, Iarumas rose from his seat. Garbage's head shot up, and she jumped to her feet to chase after him. Iarumas didn't even spare the girl a glance. His boots scraped the floor as he walked, onward and onward.

Garbage followed Iarumas, though she wasn't exactly wagging her tail, and they both left the temple.

Sister Ainikki watched them go with resignation. "I wish you a good life...and a good death."

If he lived a life that was in line with the wishes of the God that would let him die, there could be no greater happiness. If only all adventurers, and all living people, could experience such a life.

When she was finished praying for the two of them, Aine stood up. Patting down the hem of her habit, she suddenly had a thought.

"You know, I've seen that girl's face somewhere before..."

Well, it would do her no good to dwell on it. Many adventurers visited the temple. It could have been a relative or just a coincidental resemblance. Whatever the case...

He packed enough for two, I see.

That fact alone was enough to put Sister Ainikki in a good mood.

§

With his face still swollen, Raraja was miserably chewing away at a loaf of hard black bread.

It was the cheapest item on the tavern's menu, worse even than the gruel, but it was also the only thing he'd eaten in days.

His single gold coin had only fetched him a loaf of black bread.

"Damn it all...!" Raraja devoured his bread in one corner of the tavern, groaning at the pain in the corners of his mouth. Every time he opened or closed his lips to eat, his mouth stung terribly. Still, he *had* to eat. Eat or die.

This starving boy was the thief who had attacked Iarumas days earlier.

Following his party's loss, Raraja had escaped the dungeon. Alone, he'd gone running back to his clan. After all, he'd had nowhere else to go, and if he hadn't come back, they would've had him killed. But, even going back, he'd been pretty sure they would end him anyway.

Raraja was every bit the kid he looked. Just a rash young human boy—that's all he was. Regardless, both the village runt and the boy wonder with a gift for the sword would get treated the same way within the dungeon.

This kid had run off from his own village and ended up in a situation not so different from Garbage's. And now, since he'd failed to bring her back, only one thing could happen: he'd be stripped of everything out behind the tavern, then killed...like so many other nameless adventurers just starting out.

Conflict between adventurers was forbidden in town. However, if there was no struggle, then there was no problem. And if someone had never delved into the dungeon before, there would certainly be no struggle. The adventurers could make it like their victim had never existed.

But the way they'd chosen to handle Raraja was different. They'd beaten his face black and blue, and had then let him off with expulsion from the clan. It hadn't been because he was lucky, or because of his level, or anything like that. No, it'd been because Raraja didn't have a coin to his name, so they would gain nothing by killing him.

"Damn it...! Damn it...!"

It had taken him a full day to recover his hidden coin, and several days spent watching carefully, just in case his old clanmates attacked him again.

Though, once in the tavern, no one was going to take note of another seedy adventurer scarfing down a loaf of bread. And even if they did, Raraja probably had nothing to fear…considering that he had no idea what he was going to do once he finished eating the bread that his last coin had bought him.

What can I do?

His companions…were dead.

They weren't members of the clan, just people the clan had used like dogs, but he'd still been working with them. Fortunately, here in this town, it was possible to bring them back to life. Anywhere else, it would have taken a literal miracle from God.

But…Raraja could only resurrect them if he could afford the tithe.

The clan wasn't going to pay for it. They could use those guys like they were disposable because they didn't have to consider paying to resurrect them.

Since Raraja was the sole survivor, he'd have to find the money himself. But…how?

Certainly, for people like him and his associates, who hadn't lived any life worth speaking about, the cost of resurrection was low. But once you added up five people's worth, it wasn't so cheap anymore.

Raraja couldn't afford the literal miracle of raising the dead.

How could he earn money when he was just a lone thief? He couldn't kill monsters by himself—that meant no treasure boxes. He was more or less sure he'd die on either his first or second trip into the dungeon. And, if he did luck out somehow, was there any guarantee that the resurrection would even work?

No, there wasn't.

But more importantly, there was one thing that infuriated Raraja more than anything else.

"God *damn* it…!"

He knew he had to get out there and earn money…so what was he doing here, eating and drinking? That was the part of his situation that made him feel the worst.

Raraja didn't have much time left. He also had no money left. All he could do was eat the black bread in front of him, but once he did, his time was up. At that point, he'd have to enter the dungeon.

The idea of leaving Scale had never occurred to him—that's why Raraja was feeling desperate. And as he reached for his last piece of bread, he was halfway to giving in to that desperation completely.

"You there, young man," a voice said suddenly, stopping Raraja short. "Could I have a moment of your time?"

"Huh…?" Raraja hadn't meant to stop. Hadn't tried to. But there was a gentleness in that voice which compelled him. It had a mysterious power to it—a pressure. That's why it was more accurate to say that Raraja was *made* to stop, and not that he did it of his own volition.

"It seems you are in quite dire straits. If you do not mind at all, I believe I might be of some assistance."

Raraja turned a suspicious eye toward the voice. It came from an awfully well-kept man wearing a robe. *A mage?* Raraja thought. Most guys who wore robes were mages. Either that, or priests. Or else a bishop who'd mastered the arts of both.

Anyway, he hadn't expected a guy like that to start waving around a sword and lop his buddy's head off.

"Oh, you see, I myself struggled in my younger days. I couldn't bear to simply watch a young man with such promise suffer."

Before Raraja could say anything, the man sat down beside him. The thief was going to object, but the man had already put a bowl of stew in front of him.

White steam wafted from the bowl. With it, a fragrant scent. Raraja gulped.

"Consider it a token of our acquaintance. Your body is your greatest asset, you know. So please, eat up."

"R-Right…"

This man was dubious, suspicious. The words passed through Raraja's mind, then just as soon as they appeared, they mysteriously vanished.

Raraja's danger sense was tingling, but his heart refused to obey it.

Before he knew it, he'd taken the spoon in hand, and the utensil was carrying stew to his mouth. Rabbit meat. The taste of fat spread across his palate.

Delicious…

Delicious.

The moment he thought that, his hands moved. He shoveled food into his mouth like a man possessed. His belly felt warm. Delicious.

"To tell you the truth, I have a favor I would like to ask—a job that I would like you to handle."

The man's words no longer reached Raraja's ears.

A job. Money. Raraja could help his companions. Easy work. And it would let him settle his grudge.

He could no longer suspect this man or mistrust him, and he remembered just one thing from the exchange:

"You'll use this stone, you see…"

As the man pulled the stone from his pocket, Raraja noticed something hanging from his new employer's neck. A strange amulet…

No.

A broken shard of something…

§

"Why do you pounce at the monsters the moment you see them?"

"Arf?" Garbage cocked her head to the side as if she didn't know what he was talking about. She was covered head to toe in blood.

The two of them were inside a burial chamber within the dungeon. Iarumas massaged his forehead. Bodies piled up. The chamber was littered with the remains of monsters that'd had their vitals slashed, along with entrails and pools of blood.

And in the middle of the miserable scene, a treasure chest stained with dark ichor had, at some point, appeared.

The girl looked up at him like a little dog that had just picked up a ball. It was almost like she was saying, *"Here it is."*

"Woof!" Her bark sounded somewhat proud.

Iarumas opened his mouth to reply, but he closed it again without uttering a word.

I can't really blame her...

Up until now, all anyone had ever wanted from her was to kill the monsters and get the treasure chest. Hack and slash. It was one answer to the question of how to be an adventurer. But it wasn't the one Iarumas was looking for.

As Garbage scampered up to him, Iarumas peered down at her. Without hesitation, he knelt down on the bloody floor in order to look straight into those frighteningly clear eyes that were hidden deep inside her cloak.

"This time, our priority is to move on."

Garbage gave a shrill whine.

"Ignore the treasure and monsters."

She was silent.

"Do you get it?"

"Arf!"

Does she, though?

Sighing at the energetic bark she'd let out, Iarumas stood back up.

Garbage was already trotting over to the door that led out into the corridor. She turned to look at him and barked, "Ruff!"

Iarumas shouldered his heavy bag and followed her. Then, suddenly, Garbage kicked the door in.

"Arf!"

This...was more or less indicative of how things continued to be. For Iarumas, exploration was something he usually did at an almost turtle-like pace. Even on paths he knew well, ones he'd been down tens, maybe hundreds of times, he always checked things thoroughly as he moved along.

This was to avoid encountering monsters. To prevent stepping into traps. To keep himself from getting lost. He would never charge into a burial chamber, massacre everything inside, and then seize the treasure.

However, Iarumas's usual sluggish pace was something Garbage would probably never be able to tolerate. In order to survive, she killed as naturally as she breathed, and then collected treasure chests.

That was the kind of creature—the kind of adventurer—she was.

Iarumas fiddled with the Creeping Coin as he followed Garbage.

It isn't so bad.

Iarumas didn't hate exploring like this. He hadn't ever tried doing things this way simply because he couldn't have done it alone—that would've been impossible.

So, if it was possible to do it now, Iarumas had no objections.

"Hrm..."

But...

Another whine.

Once Iarumas entered the next corridor, Garbage was sitting down on the floor. He could think of several potential reasons why.

"You're hurt?"

No answer. There were no monster corpses, and the scent of blood wasn't lingering in the air. Inorganic monsters did exist in the dungeon, though, so that didn't rule out them as a possibility.

"Poison, paralysis, or petrification?"

Again, no answer. Although, each of those were horrifying ailments that would have robbed her of the ability to speak.

A long silence passed between the two of them, then...

"Hunger...or exhaustion?"

"Yap!"

It sounded like both—there was only one way to respond.

"Okay." Iarumas immediately set down his heavy pack. This was no joke. It was nothing to get exasperated or angry about. Regardless of how much visible stamina (HP) someone had left, exhaustion and hunger stalked adventurers like shadows. These ailments were always present, never leaving, sometimes frightening and ready to swallow them up if ignored.

What was so impressive about the great sages of old was that they had learned to accept their own shadows. Though, that said, Iarumas had little interest in such anecdotes. He just wanted to do what he ought to as an adventurer while he was out adventuring.

Apparently, this wasn't just *his* first long exploration in a while—it was Garbage's too.

Think about it. The people who'd kept her chained up as a meat shield had probably been satisfied as long as they could secure their loot for the day. If they'd entered burial chambers at all, it would've been just one of them, maybe two. They would have never kept progressing from one chamber to the next like this without a break.

In short…

I guess we got carried away. Both Iarumas and the girl.

That thought made the corners of Iarumas's mouth turn up ever so slightly. Heading deeper into the dungeon really was fun.

"All right, let's set up camp."

"Arf!" The girl's response was light, cheerful, and without a hint of apparent exhaustion. She watched intently as Iarumas pulled a little bottle out of his bag.

I wonder…

"Is this your first time seeing this?"

"Yap."

Yes, apparently.

However, once he pulled the cap off the bottle, she stopped twitching her nose and looked away. Its scent wasn't much to speak of, after all—it was only water.

Iarumas didn't even shrug. He simply focused on his own hands as he began pouring the water out onto the floor.

Holy water, blessed at the temple. It was a must-have for adventurers—that is, adventurers who came to this dungeon. The blessed water could be used to draw a magic circle, a barrier that would help protect those inside from some external threats.

Camp, bedding down for the night, taking a break—it didn't matter what it was called. If you were going to rest in the dungeon, holy water was a necessity. It might not do anything about the guardians in burial chambers, but it would keep the roaming monsters away.

Most importantly, Iarumas was rather fond of the process of carefully drawing a circle on the ground with water. Before they could rest, they also needed to check the ground around them. He liked that this examination was integrated into the holy water procedure. If they had survived a trap, it was entirely possible they would spring it again.

That sort of thing didn't happen because an adventurer was stupid, or inattentive. To err was human. People made mistakes. No one was perfect. Iarumas had to act on the assumption that mistakes would be made, and that's precisely why he was being cautious and drawing this magic circle with holy water.

Checking the floor secured their safety, the process of pouring out the holy water helped him to settle down, and taking a break would give him rest.

Yes, people do make mistakes.

Garbage whined again, feeling rather too hungry and tired. Iarumas had let his guard down just a little. This was a corridor, so there were no guardians here. And as for an encounter with wandering monsters, he didn't hear any footsteps.

And that was why—

"Hrm…!" Iarumas grunted. Garbage's head suddenly shot up.

—they were a moment too slow to react to the shadow that shot out of the dungeon's darkness.

Unfortunately, a moment was all this shadow needed.

The dark shape ran soundlessly across the stone floor, treading over the circle of holy water and pulling a stone from his pocket. Iarumas recognized the spell dancing on the parchment that the shadow unfurled. His eyes widened.

"You fool, that's…!"

Dangerous, perhaps? Was that what he'd tried to say?

There was no way to know now—it made little difference.

A blinding light flooded out of the broken stone, engulfing the three of them as if it were whiting everything out.

Iarumas, Garbage, and—though this goes without saying—Raraja.

When the white flash that swallowed them subsided, all three had vanished. All that was left was a bottle on the ground, bed mats, a trampled magic circle, and shards of stone.

That was it.

All of it would be carried off by passing monsters. No trace would linger for much longer.

Had magic blown them to smithereens?

Or had it dissolved them into ash and dust?

Or perhaps…

§

"Huh?! Ah?!" Raraja blinked. Unable to understand what'd just happened, he shouted, "Where the hell is this?!"

Somewhere in the darkness, a low voice answered, "You should be grateful we're not inside the rock, at least." The voice was clearheaded, unemotional.

Raraja's mind and vision were hazy. He blinked repeatedly, rubbing his face.

"Wahhhhhh, Iarumas?!"

"Arf."

"Garbage?!"

The girl barked as if to say, *"I'm here too."* Those cold blue eyes deep within her cloak made Raraja recoil in fear.

A-Am I gonna die…?!

Obviously, he wasn't emotionally prepared to do so. When a person became an adventurer, they only imagined how things were going to work out for them. *I'm different,* they'd think. *I can get myself out of any jam.* Did the possibility of death feel real to them? No. Of course not.

If it had, they could have never explored the dungeon.

That's why, at that moment, Raraja was being driven by two thoughts: *"Oh, shit."* and *"I don't wanna die."*

He reflexively jumped back, hand flashing to the dagger at his waist and body sinking into a defensive posture.

The dungeon? He looked around. This was an unfamiliar burial chamber, but he was still inside the dungeon—that much he was certain of. *Was I kidnapped?*

"A-Are you gonna kill me?!"

Retribution. That was the word that came to Raraja's mind. Like he— no, his former clan—had tried to take against the pair in front of him.

These two could enact their revenge here in the dungeon.

But Iarumas's response was unlike any adventurer's he'd met before.

"It takes guts, delving into the dungeon as a lone thief," he said plainly. Then, with what sounded like pure curiosity, he asked. "Where did you get your hands on that?"

"Huh...?"

"The stone," came Iarumas's simple reply. "I didn't know that anyone had the Demon's Stone in these parts."

"Uh, no, I-I..." Raraja stammered before gulping, overcome by the pressure.

It was bizarre. He sensed something—something inscrutable—in the glare of the fire that burned in Iarumas's eyes.

Raraja's voice trembled as he desperately traced his memories back. Then, falteringly, he began to put words together. "In the tavern, I was eating, and then...there was a strange man... He spoke to me..."

What happened next?

"A strange man, you say?"

Raraja nodded. "A mage, I think... Around his neck, he had this weird..." He searched for the word. "Amulet...thing. Like a shard of something."

"An amulet?"

Raraja had no immediate answer.

Iarumas was smiling. It was a broad, dark grin. One so wide that it looked as though the corners of his mouth might tear.

"You—what's your name?"

"Ra—" His voice cracked. "Rara...ja."

"I see." Iarumas stood up. The Ring of Jewels that he wore over the top of his black gauntlet was sparkling.

"Dauk mimuarif peiche (*O cloth, spread out, show my place*)," he chanted.

Raraja felt something unseen—like the wind—softly brush against his cheek.

Considering the startled "Yap?!" from Garbage—who was next to Iarumas, waiting—Raraja wasn't just imagining it.

It's a spell.

Raraja knew instinctively. It was the location spell, DUMAPIC.

He knew it. This guy *was* a mage. A mage who could use a sword...

"Well, we're still on the same level," Iarumas concluded, "but I see that we were sent a long way away." He reached into his pocket and pulled out a coin, then threw it out of the burial chamber and into the corridor. When it landed, he reeled it back in and walked off without a word. Garbage trotted off after him.

"Huh?"

That just left Raraja. He hadn't recovered from his confusion yet, but...

"H-Hey!" If nothing else, he'd managed to stutter that out to Iarumas. Though, he regretted the word once it'd left his mouth.

Confusion—fear—relief.

Not getting killed—being left behind—this man going away.

Iarumas heard all of these sentiments mixed into the voice that had called after him, He turned to look at Raraja over his shoulder.

"What, you aren't coming along?" Bizarrely, his voice was full of cheer. "You don't get an adventure like this very often."

Raraja couldn't resist.

§

Clink, clink. A gold coin bounced along.

The man in black who'd thrown the coin reeled it back in with the connected fishing line, then threw it out again.

Raraja followed him through the darkness of the dungeon, not knowing where they were headed.

Here in the dungeon, there seemed to be no sense of time, even though it was passing. Had they walked for an hour? Half an hour? Minutes? In the midst of that vague passage of time, Raraja observed and discovered one thing:

This guy's ability to explore—in other words, his skill as a thief—is nothing to write home about.

That was the conclusion Raraja came to while following Iarumas. Yes, the man had some impressive tricks. That Creeping Coin of his wasn't one that Raraja had known about. And the way he moved... It wasn't clear whether he was a fighter or a mage, but whatever role he filled, he was good at it.

However, when it came to pure exploration...Raraja couldn't rate Iarumas all that highly.

He was cautious. But not like a thief.

He avoided traps. Okay, that made sense. But he was avoiding treasure chests too. Which meant...

This guy can't *disable traps.*

"Arf!"

The bark came from behind Raraja and made him jump a little. *Quit woolgathering!* implied the bark. Or maybe, *Get going already.* It had to mean something like that.

Looking over his shoulder, Raraja locked eyes with the monsters' leftovers—Garbage. She looked upset.

Raraja quickened his pace, fearing those clear blue eyes that seemed to suck him in. He closed the distance to Iarumas. The back bobbing in front of him belonged to an adventurer who just happened to be a little cautious.

But...

If I jumped him, I doubt I could kill him.

Raraja didn't have any intention of killing the man anyway, but if, for sake of argument, he were to try...well, he could imagine that his head would fly for it.

That, or he'd split my torso clean in two.

Raraja shuddered, a shrill voice escaping from his throat as he tried to kill his fear.

"Hey..." murmured Raraja.

"What?" Iarumas didn't turn. The coin bounced across the floor, and then he reeled it back in.

"What was that thing?"

"The Demon's Stone, you mean?"

Iarumas knew about it, then. Raraja thought he detected a hint of fond remembrance in that voice. But, had Raraja been standing in front of the man instead of behind him, he would have known otherwise—Iarumas's expression was one of confusion about *what* exactly he was feeling nostalgic about.

"When shattered, it turns everyone around it to ash."

"Whuh?!" Raraja cried. Perhaps amused by his reaction, Iarumas stopped and turned to look at him.

Turned to ash. As far as Raraja was concerned, that meant death. No one would resurrect him. A permanent end.

"If used well, it teleports people instead," Iarumas continued. "Though, I don't know if the one you had was incomplete, or if you just used it well."

It must've been defective, Raraja concluded. He'd never done anything "well" in his life. And he wasn't going to start now—not when he was being used as someone's errand boy.

"The guy must hate you pretty bad, huh?"

"Could be," Iarumas muttered.

Reduced to ash—the dust of the dungeon. An adventurer would be tread upon by monsters, scattered, and lost. It was a truly horrifying thought, one Raraja didn't even want to imagine. If an enemy who wanted to do that to *him* ever appeared, he'd either run away or get down on his knees and beg.

Yet Iarumas was impassive, as though it was no big deal to him.

Maybe!

In truth, Raraja had no idea what went through the man's head. And there was one more thing he didn't understand: Raraja couldn't figure out why he was still alive.

With a sideward glance at Garbage, who let out a bored whine behind him, Raraja cautiously decided to ask the question. He lowered his hips so that he could run at any time—not that he was convinced it would do him any good.

"You're not...gonna kill me?"

"Inside the dungeon, it's not so uncommon for adventurers of differing alignments to work together," responded Iarumas.

The answer was simple.

Iarumas walked on without looking back at Raraja. He threw the coin and reeled it in again, then walked some more. He would occasionally stop, let his Ring of Jewels shine as he checked their location, and write something down on parchment. This parchment had a graph carved into it, and when Raraja stole a glimpse of it, he could immediately tell that it was a map.

But could Iarumas follow it to get back to the surface? Raraja certainly couldn't.

Ultimately, Raraja's only chance of survival was to follow this strange man in black.

That's why, having already asked one question, he decided to keep the conversation going. However, he didn't want to offend the man. The image of his comrade's head getting lopped off was still stuck in his mind.

"Well, I'm sure it happens, but…"

Alignment… It wasn't such a rigid thing. It was merely a matter of the way a person tended to behave—whether they avoided unnecessary battles, whether they allowed wounded enemies to live, or whether they'd put their fellow party members before themselves. The smallest of choices could be the difference between life and death in the dungeon, so there was no time to debate beliefs in the middle of exploring.

As such, it was far better to group up with people who shared the same general policy. Especially since, up on the surface, disputes between adventurers (open ones, at least) were forbidden. That was why it was best for those of differing alignments not to get involved with one another.

There were those who referred to alignments with big, important-sounding words like *lawful* and *chaotic*, *good* and *evil*, but…

It's all absurd.

Raraja snorted.

As for the difference between these terms, well, it probably wasn't any deeper than whether a person would help others without compensation or not. Chaotic or evil—people who'd help you but then demand money, or people who'd just leave you to rot. These labels were just what you called guys like that.

Guys like the ones in his clan who'd taken advantage of him… Or maybe even Raraja himself, since he'd been so willing to follow his clan mates.

But…was his alignment actually different from the others here?

"Since you're a corpse retriever and all…I figured you were probably on the same side as me."

"I try to stay neutral," said Iarumas. "As for her…"

"Arf?"

"Who knows…?"

Raraja looked behind him at the girl who seemed to have no idea what they were talking about. She looked totally out of it—uninterested in other people—but kept on following Iarumas. Regardless of whether you decided to classify Garbage as lawful or chaotic, the other members of those alignments wouldn't know what to do with her.

Ultimately, alignment's really not that big of a deal, huh?

Raraja was busy thinking about this, and maybe that's why he almost missed it when Iarumas continued, murmuring, "Besides, you're not the one who's my enemy."

And with that, the man closed his mouth.

Faint footsteps. The *clink, clink* of the coin. The sound of string being reeled in. More footsteps.

What's he thinking…?

If it were up to Raraja's judgment—or, if guys like the ones who'd taken advantage of him were making the decision—Raraja's life would've been forfeit after his failed attack on Iarumas. And if, for some reason, they did let him live, it would only be so they could use him as a living ten-foot pole (not that he'd ever seen a real one). Basically, they'd fatten him up for use as a meat shield and trap disarmer. Or…something like that.

Raraja could only imagine two reasons why he'd been allowed to live: one, this man in black was plotting something, or two, he just didn't care one way or the other.

Iarumas had said it was the latter, but Raraja wasn't going to take that at face value. If the kid were that credulous, he'd have been turned into another corpse out behind the tavern a long time ago.

What the hell's he thinking…?

Raraja couldn't even guess.

The suspicious man from the tavern. A strange scroll. The depths of the dungeon. The inscrutable pair he was now traveling with.

Even if Raraja managed to get back to town, was he going to be all right? He didn't know. Maybe there'd be retribution from the man who'd hired him. Or perhaps, his former clan mates would decide to execute him.

The more Raraja thought about it, the more the possibilities swirled around in his head, just feeding his baseless sense of unease…and the dungeon wasn't so safe that he could afford to wander around in a distracted state.

Basically, it's all about money.

In the end, things were a little easier for him if he chose to think in terms of money. Raraja concluded that all this was about the coin he'd be paying to get his buddies resurrected.

If I'm dead, there won't be anyone left to pay to revive them—there'd be no tithe, and that's a loss for him. Iarumas probably had a contract with the temple or something, so he'd want to avoid that outcome.

Obviously, though, Raraja wasn't optimistic enough to fully convince himself of that fact.

"Woof!"

Without meaning to, Raraja had stopped walking. Garbage barked at him to hurry up, making him jump a little.

"O-Okay! Okay! I get it. Don't rush me!"

Raraja followed Iarumas, and the low growl from behind urged him on.

They kept moving forward.

The darkness of the dungeon. Monsters. Traps. The man in front. The girl in back. Troubles on the surface.

Raraja didn't know which of these was the least of his problems, but for now, he was alive. *I've got to cling to that.* This was the one thing Raraja was certain of, even if he had no idea what was going on.

However, the dungeon was not a place where things stayed uneventful for long. A short time later, Raraja would run into something and be forced to stop. This obstacle just so happened to be…

"A door…"

Was it a great iron door looming over him? Or a wooden door no taller than Raraja? Here in the dungeon, perception was vague. If he didn't focus, then the structure of the door became fuzzy.

Only one thing was certain—there *was* a door.

Though the history of the dungeon remained unclear, this feature was one of the things that proved it must be man-made.

"Woof!"

Garbage looked ready to charge through, but Iarumas seized her by the scruff of the neck. "I've never explored this area before," he muttered, "so here's hoping that the other side is familiar territory."

"We're going through…?" Raraja asked.

"Even if we tried to find another way, there's no telling what we might run into," Iarumas replied.

Raraja gulped. Hopefully, there was a hallway on the other side.

Because, in a burial chamber…there were guaranteed to be monsters lying in wait. And if there were…

We might die.

One of Raraja's hands unconsciously felt for the daggers on his belt. They were thin, brittle blades, hardly fit to be called weapons. He'd needed to argue hard—claiming he required them to disarm traps— before he'd been allowed to carry them for self-defense. It had been a spot of good luck that he'd managed to get away from the clan without having them confiscated. Raraja hoped that luck would keep up.

"S-So…we're going in?" The tone of Raraja's question was different now.

"Yeah," Iarumas replied, with a short nod. He reached under his cloak to the black rod hanging from his belt and used his thumb to loosen the thin saber slightly from its scabbard.

The echo of the metallic click felt loud and unpleasant.

"Okay."

"Woof!"

The moment Iarumas let go of her, Garbage barked and charged in. She was like a colored gust of wind, kicking through the door and surging forward on pure inertia. Iarumas followed her like a shadow, while Raraja hurriedly chased after the two of them. They weren't well coordinated. But this was how adventurers moved, and it was faster than any awkward attempts at coordination. That's how they were able to act before their opponent—a massive thing squatting in the middle of the burial chamber.

Wh-What's that…?! Raraja's eyes went wide.

"Grrruff!" Garbage let out a low growl.

Bluish green scales. A slimy tongue that glistened with saliva. Burning red eyes. Fangs. Claws. A tail. The things on its back that looked like thorns were a pair of wings, spread wide. It rose up on four legs.

Boom. The burial chamber seemed to shudder. Terrifying. Raraja felt his knees shaking, his legs starting to give out.

He managed to stay on his feet, but not due to any sort of bravery. If he ran—moved—backed down—he'd be killed, and he could sense that instinctively.

It was a vague outline. Its true form, indistinct. Yet, there was no need to second-guess what it was. Any adventurer could tell you—even a child could.

"A d-dragon…?!" Raraja stammered.

"No," Iarumas replied, smiling. "A gas dragon."

§

The head rose up slowly, spewing noxious, rotting breath that filled the air with a sulfurous stench. It didn't look friendly. There was no avoiding a battle at this point.

Of course, that didn't mean Raraja thought they could take on a dragon. The best he could manage was to hold his dagger in a backhand grip, tight as he could, and try to stay on his feet somehow.

His eyes, wide with disbelief, were on the dragon…and Iarumas.

"Hmm… So they *can* show up here." Iarumas was smiling, an expression of true delight…almost like how someone might grin when unexpectedly running into an old friend.

For the first time, Raraja felt like he could sympathize with Garbage, who was right beside him, growling. Distance-wise, she was closer to him than the man in black…

"Urkh…?!"

That's when it happened.

Raraja's five senses, which had been honed at least somewhat by his days of work as a thief, warned him that something was off.

Bzzz.

A low, timorous sound—small and thin, but unpleasant. The beating of wings.

Insects? Winged ones? No...

"Whuh—aghhh?!"

"Yap?!"

Instinctively, Raraja dove to the side, taking Garbage with him. Several strands of hair flew through the air.

Raraja knew, intuitively, that they'd been bitten off...by the massive, ominous insect with the killer jaws that had just buzzed past his and Garbage's heads.

That thing, which looked like something out of a nightmare, was definitely a monster.

"A giant dragonfly...?!"

Obviously, even Garbage winced at this, letting out a shocked, questioning whine. But Raraja had figured something out: his fear of the dragon felt unreal, but his hatred of the dragonfly was all too real.

Though, obviously, the imposing dragon deeper in the room was a greater threat than the dragonfly buzzing around them.

"They use breath weapons," Iarumas warned, his drawn sword in his right hand. He used the same tone one might use to advise someone that it would rain, so they should bring an umbrella. "A fighter might be able to withstand it, but a thief like you doesn't stand a chance."

"Just telling me to be careful doesn't help!"

Raraja had no clue what to do. Normally, he'd get told to charge in and act as a shield for the others, or something like that. That was all Raraja knew how to do.

Garbage was more or less the same. They called her the monster's leftovers because she'd survived doing it.

Raraja was, thus, forced to look to Iarumas. The man was shuffling toward the gas dragon, keeping close track of the distance between himself and the monster.

"You focus on parrying," Iarumas ordered.

Raraja nodded. "G-Got it...!" He turned toward the dragonflies with a level of obedience that stunned even himself.

Just how many were there buzzing around? Raraja's brow was greasy with sweat as he squinted at them.

Whatever, this beats taking on the real *dragon!* If Iarumas was saying he could do something about that thing, then Raraja would just have to pray it would be enough. He felt no guilt whatsoever for shoving the task off on Iarumas. After all, he already had his hands full with these dragonflies.

"Let's do this."

"Arf!"

He had been talking to himself, not giving an order, but Garbage charged straight at the enemy. She seemed to fly over Raraja's head, swinging her broadsword. Her target: the green gas dragon.

The blitz attack seemed to catch the dragon off guard. Its fresh blood splashed through the darkness.

"GRROOOOOOAAAAAAARRRR!!!"

"Yap?!"

But that was all.

Having had some scales knocked off its forehead, the creature roared right in Garbage's face, making her squeak out a terrified yelp. As the dragon's fangs bore down on her, the girl kicked it in the snout and rolled out of the way.

Yeah, Garbage definitely has talent, thought Raraja. *She might even be a genius.*

The difference between her and him was night and day—she must have received more of the blessings of the Gods (bonus points) than he had.

But that didn't change their current situation.

We come up short in everything…! Levels, equipment, experience— all of it.

Neither of them could truly take on a dragon.

"BZZZZZZZZZZ!!!"

"Wah? Ahhh?!"

Raraja couldn't afford to keep close track of Garbage's movements any longer. It wasn't easy to fend off the dragonflies and the hateful buzzing of their wings. Raraja had never done it before, at least.

"Get away from me! Back off, damn it!!!" Raraja swung his dagger at buzzing dragonflies, not so much as an attack, but to drive them off.

The only monsters Raraja had ever fought before now had been on the shallow floors. Orcs and kobolds were about all he could manage, and even those were unbelievably frightening to someone from the surface.

Still, though…

They're fast!

The dragonflies were too quick for Raraja's eyes to follow. He had to listen closely to the buzzing of their wings, and even then, the best he could manage was to narrowly deflect their attacks with his dagger.

"Wagh?!"

Sparks flew through the dungeon each time his blade struck their jaws, the incredible force of the blow knocking his arm back.

Sharp pain shot through his dagger hand. He wasn't wearing armor. The pain was numbing him.

"That! Hurts!!! Damn! You!!!"

Still, it was better than it could have been. Iarumas had said that they had a breath attack.

They?

That meant the dragon…*and* the dragonflies.

Raraja only knew about dragon's breath from the bedtime stories he'd been told as a young boy. A younger him had dreamed of seeing it one day. The current him, however, had one little addendum to make to that wish…

To see it…from as far away as possible.

Without that stipulation, his teeth would start chattering, and he might burst out in nervous laughter at any moment.

"Grrr!" Raraja gritted his teeth, turning up the corners of his lips as he held his dagger at the ready. He focused on the dragonflies' jaws— whether they were coming in for a bite, or about to spew fire.

That was why he was able to react to the sudden bout of blue-white flames—

"Whoa, that's hot…?!"

—and dodge just in time.

He bent over backward to get out of the way. The flames grazed the tip of his nose, singeing his bangs and leaving behind a nasty smell.

Raraja fell on his back, screaming like a madman as he rolled directly to one side—the dragonflies were coming at him like a hail of arrows from above. The sound of their sharp fangs tearing into the stone floor where he'd been moments ago warned him that his defenses would be useless.

He'd narrowly survived. But there was limited space inside the burial chamber. If he didn't have time to get back up, then the result was going to be the same.

"Arf!"

Of course, this might've been the case...had Raraja been alone.

But Garbage went on the offensive, cutting down those annoying dragonflies that wouldn't leave him alone. She relied on brute force—no, on putting the full weight of her body behind her broadsword—as she danced through the air.

Her blade, with the added momentum of her spin behind it, tore right through a dragonfly's carapace.

"Thanks, you saved me!"

"Yap!" Garbage barked, seemingly unbothered by the chunks of wings and the filthy bug juice raining down on them. The bark probably wasn't a response to what he'd said—her eyes were already focused on her next quarry.

So, the thanks had only been for Raraja's sake. Regardless, he wouldn't have felt right not saying it.

He put his hands on the ground and bounded to his feet, dagger in one hand. For now at least, he needed to defend himself...

"Whoa?!"

But before he had time to finish thinking that, Raraja's field of vision was engulfed by an intense white flash. All he could do was cover his face. Meanwhile, right beside him, Garbage began screaming incoherently.

There was a horrible stench, a heat, and the sting of burning flesh. But that was it.

Raraja didn't have to look to figure out that it was the gas dragon's breath. He *did*, however, try to peek through the gap between his arms. He had to know.

What was that man—Iarumas—doing?

§

Iarumas was alive, standing before the gas dragon, katana held loosely at his side.

Okay, I know I said I'd do this, but...

How to attack? He'd have to figure that out as he went.

"ROOAAARRR!!!"

Claws—the claws were coming at him. Claws and fangs. Iarumas skillfully dodged, slipping past them.

Dragons were legendary beasts on the surface, but here in the dungeon? Not so much. Iarumas remembered that fact, though he'd forgotten where or when he'd learned it.

Yes, down in the dungeon, this green-scaled dragon was considered a weak enemy, not even a medium-level threat... Still, it wasn't good to let it grind down his focus (HP) like this.

It was even worse for the other two, who were both a lower level than Iarumas was.

Adventuring in an unexplored region of the dungeon would be a source of experience for them, but only if they could settle down and reflect on what they'd seen. In short, until they all got back to the surface alive—or, until at least one member of their party made it back to resurrect the rest—it was meaningless.

Still holding his katana loosely in his right hand, Iarumas began forming magical signs with his left.

He had only one option   spells.

Caught up in the illusion of having infinite time between moves, he opened the spell book inside his head.

HALITO is not going to cut it...

Fire might have been the natural enemy of the gas dragon, but the *weakest* fire spell wasn't going to work. MAHALITO wouldn't either. LAHALITO might—but there was no guarantee. He could use

CORTU to put up a magic screen or BACORTU to fizzle its breath weapon, but…

I don't need to play the long game like that.

"I'll do this the good old-fashioned way…" Iarumas muttered. The gas dragon roared, though probably not because it'd heard him.

No adventurer in this dungeon feared a dragon's roar.

As it cried out, the dragon swung down with its claws. Iarumas wasn't going to be an idiot and try to block those talons and their steel-rending sharpness. He was holding his katana, the blade resting on his right shoulder, and he used it to turn the attack aside, stepping inside the dragon's reach with the same motion.

Opening jaws. Sharp fangs. The smell of sulfur on its breath. White light in the back of its throat.

Iarumas noticed all of this—the signs of his impending death—but simply accepted them with a, "Yeah, that's about right."

The dragon had been watching Iarumas too. Its burning eyes were focused on the white blade he swung.

The corners of Iarumas's mouth turned up ever so slightly. Words of true power raced from his lips. The words turned to hot, white light, whirling into a roaring vortex as the lightning spell came together.

"Zearif laikaf (*O, Fist of God*)!!!"

Iarumas's left hand crackled with electricity as he pounded it into the gas dragon's jaw.

"GRRROOAAARGGGG?!?!?!"

The thunderous rumble of his uppercut connecting was, obviously, not because of Iarumas's own strength.

It was TZALIK, the Fist of God, one of the very few mage spells that invoked the name of the divine.

This blow unleashed God's might—lightning pierced through the gas dragon's entire body, burning it to a crisp. The incredible power shook the air as it slew the dragon… It was the stuff of myths. Tzalik was a fourth-level spell, only putting it in the middle tier of all the spells cast in the dungeon. However…

It requires the caster to touch their target, so no proper mage is going to want to use it.

The dragon—its body half turned to ash—bubbled and let off putrid smoke before finally falling to the ground.

Ignoring the way the burial chamber shook with the impact, and how Raraja was gaping at him in disbelief, Iarumas simply murmured, "Moving on…"

His eyes were on just one thing—the blood-soaked treasure chest in the corner of the chamber.

§

"I-Is it over…?" Raraja asked, hesitantly crawling out to check.

"No, not yet," Iarumas replied.

"Arf!" Garbage barked. She strode over to the treasure chest, snorting proudly and puffing her chest up with pride, almost as if she had found it herself.

"Yelp! Yelp!"

"Don't touch it," Iarumas warned. At this point, he was entirely *too* accustomed to how hasty the girl could be when she got excited.

Garbage obeyed him, albeit reluctantly. Though, it wasn't that she understood why—Iarumas said not to do it, so she wouldn't. She was probably just waiting.

As Raraja watched this exchange vacantly, Iarumas suddenly said something unbelievable.

"Well? This is your job, isn't it?"

"Huh…?" Raraja blinked. Repeatedly. He reexamined the situation, mulling over the words he'd just heard to see if he was missing something. Nothing came to mind. He still didn't comprehend it.

"At a time like this…you wanna deal with a treasure chest?" asked Raraja.

"I don't understand."

Raraja had asked the question, just to check, but Iarumas's reply was something he himself had wanted to say.

Iarumas stood next to the treasure chest, his posture relaxed. "Why would we ignore a chest," he continued, "when we have a thief in the party?"

Raraja had no response. Iarumas had said it almost like he was asking someone why they wouldn't eat if they were hungry. Now, Raraja could see that this was common sense to Iarumas—the man couldn't imagine a thief *not* opening the treasure chest.

"Y-You're not worried I might…" Raraja's brain raced, searching for the words, "set off the trap, wiping us all out?"

Ultimately, what came out of his mouth was a lack of confidence in his own abilities.

Iarumas's response, unlike Raraja's, was totally unshaken. "If it's a poison needle or a stunner, you're the one who'll get hit, and if it's an exploding box, well, *I* probably won't die."

And as long as *he* didn't die, he could haul the corpses back to the temple to be resurrected. That's what Iarumas was saying. Raraja blinked repeatedly. Garbage let out a small yawn.

Here in the dungeon, death wasn't the end. Raraja knew that. He did. But…

Is that something you can just accept…?

He wasn't so sure. No, the attitude this man possessed went beyond acceptance. Accepting meant internalizing some piece of common sense that was external to your own. But this man, Iarumas—the way he acted was almost like one of the dungeon's monsters. He was steeped in the ways of dungeon life. They came to him as easy as breathing.

Seriously… Is this guy really the same kind of creature as me?

"Well, I'll give it a go," Raraja said, "but don't get your hopes up."

"Don't worry. We won't know if the items are valuable or not until we take them back to town for identification."

Yeah, no… That's not what I meant.

Raraja might have looked like he had a choice, but that wasn't really the case. Once he realized that, his lips twisted into a cynical smile—even he didn't know whether it was out of self-mockery or fear.

No different from usual, right?

He pulled the familiar tools from his belt, cheap wire ones he'd gotten his hands on without the guys in his clan noticing.

In front of him was the treasure chest—silent and unmoving.

"Whew…"

First, he took a deep breath, holding his knife in his right hand. He swung it as if slashing the area around the chest.

He didn't feel anything. *Nothing on the outside.*

Next, Raraja crouched in front of the box. He took an especially flat tool from his set, which looked a bit like a metal file. He slowly inserted it in the gap between the box and the lid, then cautiously worked it all the way around.

If there was a string tying the lid to the box, he'd find it this way.

It looked like the lid wasn't going to uncork an explosive bottle or pull the trigger on a crossbow trap when he opened it.

"You're used to this," Iarumas remarked.

Raraja scowled. "Is that sarcasm…?"

"It's a simple observation. You're good for someone of your level."

Raraja didn't respond.

No one had taught him the trade. The thief class was one you got pushed into if you were lightweight or small, so…

Ultimately, you're just a shield.

They had never been counting on him to disarm traps. His clan mates had only wanted him to be light on his feet and take hits for them. That was all.

There had been other guys like him, full of baseless hopes that they could make something of themselves in the dungeon. Eventually, though, they'd gotten caught by the clan and used as meat shields…

Those guys had died, one after another—blown away, or left to rot in a burial chamber after being poisoned or paralyzed.

Raraja had watched them desperately as he'd waited for his turn to come around. After all, his life had been literally on the line. He'd seen how his comrades (not those bastards in the clan, his *real* comrades) had died, and he did his best to remember what'd killed them—which traps, and how they'd messed up.

Needles around the outside of the treasure chest. Strings between the lid and the box.

He'd also seen firsthand that you could die with a crossbow bolt through your brainpan if you were dumb enough to look into the keyhole. That time, it'd been a little rhea girl. She'd said she was there to earn money to send to her parents back home.

Even after being thrown to the clan, she'd still acted exuberant, often singing to herself. Raraja'd always thought she had a pretty voice.

Though, a blood-choked gurgle was the last he'd heard of it.

When she'd fallen on her back, convulsing, an arrow freshly sprouted from her forehead, her eye had turned toward him for a brief moment. But then someone had booted her in the head, kicking her off to the corner of the burial chamber like some sort of ball. They'd cackled, stripping her of all items.

Then, they'd turned to Raraja.

"You're next."

He still didn't know how much experience he'd gotten from watching. But what he did know for certain was...that he'd survived to this day.

And that her body was still lying there in that burial chamber.

"O...kay..."

Having checked thoroughly around the chest, inspecting the box and the lid, Raraja determined that those components weren't rigged with traps. However, he couldn't let his guard down—he now had to contend with the keyhole. Raraja wiped his sweat away and went to work.

He could hear Garbage whining behind him out of boredom.

At this point, Raraja had separated his mind from his hands. It wasn't that he'd lost focus on his task—on the contrary, Raraja enjoyed picking locks. The mechanism in front of him moved when he moved it. A straightforward device.

As he was operating it, loosening it up... Well, he didn't exactly know how to describe the sensation, but it let him stop thinking about other things.

His current situation—the girl who'd died—his murdered companions and the man who'd killed them.

His client.

The chest's lock rattled as he cautiously moved his hands. As he worked, a word slipped out of Raraja's mouth.

"Hey."

"Yeah."

He hadn't been expecting a response, but Iarumas obliged him.

Speaking of being obliging—Raraja hadn't sensed the man moving farther back while he worked on the trap. Iarumas was still waiting close by while Raraja dealt with the chest. Garbage was too.

Is this what it's like being in a party?

A party? This? The three of them, who had just been thrown together by circumstance?

The thought made him a little happy. After thinking for a moment, Raraja asked a question. "If I told you the world is flat, and the edge is a steep cliff, but I want to go beyond it...would you laugh?"

"We all venture for our own reasons..."

Raraja felt one of the mechanisms click into place as he waited for Iarumas to say more.

This man was an adventurer.

He wasn't sure what defined an adventurer. But he knew that the guys in the clan didn't live up to the label. That was for sure. Raraja wanted to hear how a true adventurer would respond.

"Money...or power." Iarumas's words came out falteringly inside the burial chamber. "Some want the Lord's Garb, or cursed swords, or other strange weapons... I've known guys like that."

The dungeon was awfully quiet. The only sounds came from Raraja's picking, Garbage's sniffing...and Iarumas, talking at his slow, relaxed pace.

"The important thing is whether you go into the dungeon, or not. Whether you venture, or not. That's all."

"Even for guys who throw away rookies to do it?" Raraja asked.

"I've never thought about that," Iarumas answered easily. "I've got my hands full with my own adventure."

"Your own adventure..."

Raraja felt a little resistance on his pick. He flipped the pin. The tumbler fell into place.

He continued, carefully setting them one by one.

This was no different from Iarumas throwing his coin and reeling it back in—Raraja was checking that things were safe, then moving on to the next step.

"You've got an objective?" Raraja asked.

"I do." Iarumas smiled. "Not that you'd believe me if I told you."

Raraja opened his mouth to ask what it was, but at that moment, there was a heavy clunk as the lid fell.

He'd successfully unlocked the chest.

"Arf!!!"

"Whoa…?!"

Garbage practically pushed Raraja out of the way as she pounced on the treasure chest, barking eagerly as she peered inside. Raraja hadn't gotten a proper look in there yet, but he didn't have the energy to get mad at her. Instead, he let out an exhausted sigh and rubbed his forehead, which was thick with sweat.

"Well done," Iarumas remarked, congratulating him.

After a moment of sullen silence, Raraja said, "Getting a compliment from you isn't gonna make me feel any better."

And yet, there it was. A certain feeling of satisfaction—accomplishment. He was overjoyed to have done his job, won his battle.

Though, that feeling lessened somewhat over the course of the five or six more chests that he had to open on the way back to the surface.

§

The world shone with the color of gold.

Not metaphorically.

The light the sun cast as it was touching the horizon made everything look more beautiful.

The dungeon, and the town around it, were steeped in pale colors that made them look like some kind of golden temple.

Raraja paused for a moment, unable to tell if it was sunrise or sunset. After a moment, he became sure that dusk was imminent—the sun set in the west, and rose in the east.

But, he didn't know *when* this sunset was.

Was it still the same day they'd delved into the dungeon? The day after? Had three days passed? A week—a month—a year…? Four decades? Several centuries?

Time felt different, uncertain, when traveling between the dungeon and the surface.

"We…made it back…"

"Arf…"

Any sense of accomplishment or excitement he'd felt had long since vanished. All that remained was a sluggish feeling of exhaustion.

His life was no longer at risk—from traps or monsters, at least. That fact alone was more than enough for Raraja.

It went without saying—the only reason Garbage was tired was that she'd gotten too carried away while celebrating.

"It's not over yet," Iarumas said, poking Raraja in the back. His demeanor remained unchanged. "We need to find a bishop at the tavern to identify our haul, or we won't turn much of a profit."

"At the *tavern*…?" Raraja echoed, incredulous.

"If we have the weapon shop to do it, they'll rob us blind." Iarumas let out a rumbling laugh after he said this, but it wasn't clear what was so funny about it. Behind him were the pieces of equipment they'd been able to retrieve on the way out of the dungeon and more bags swollen with luggage.

Raraja knew that those bags had originally been meant for lugging back corpses…but he lacked the will to say anything about it. The weight of the goods filling the bag he carried dug into his shoulder like the claws of the dead. And, in order to escape from it, he wanted to get back to the inn as soon as possible…and sleep in the stables.

He'd never imagined the day would come when he would long for the feeling of straw against his cheek so badly!

But…

Even if staying in the stables was free, food still cost money. Money Raraja didn't have. If he didn't venture to the tavern, he'd probably go hungry tomorrow.

After a long, resigned silence, Raraja finally conceded. "I'll go. I'll go, okay?"

Just as Raraja accepted that he had to do it—

"Hey, what's up? You miss out on some money?"

—a voice that sounded far too cheerful for the dungeon came from behind them like a slap on the back.

Raraja turned around, surprised. Behind him was a party of six people...no, five people and one body.

The man at the lead of the group (who wore a dragon helmet) had a sack—a body bag—slung over his shoulder. "Bet you're pretty disappointed," the man remarked, "bringing back a couple of living kids instead of some dead guys."

"Wish I had your luck," Iarumas said. "Is it Hawk that's dead?"

"Even if you killed that idiot, he'd still come back," answered the elven woman behind the fighter.

A priest... Raraja could tell from her outfit.

A fighter with a dragon helmet. A female elven priest. And...

A dwarven bishop. "Our thief opened a chest thinking it had a poison needle trap, but turns out, it was an exploding box, y'see. What a shame."

A human mage. "It always goes like this when we team up with anyone but Hawkwind. It's a real problem."

A rhea thief. "One of the junior adventurers asked me to help train him, but, yeah...it didn't go so well. I feel kinda bad about it."

Each joined the conversation, one after another.

However, it was the name "Hawkwind" that was the deciding factor for Raraja. Any thief who worked in Scale, no matter how lowly, would have heard his name at least once. Raraja knew it, even if only barely. Which meant this party was...

Sezmar's party...?!

"H-He knows them?!" Raraja asked in a hushed voice, shocked that the man in black had such connections. He only got a disinterested bark from Garbage in response.

Picked the wrong person to ask...

But Raraja lacked the courage to butt into a conversation between first-rate adventurers.

The elven woman, Sarah, looked at Raraja and Garbage with a cat-like grin.

"So, Iarumas, I heard from Aine. You finally put together a party?" Sarah came toward them. Her curiosity was readily apparent by the way her eyes sparkled and her ears, so similar to bamboo leaves, swayed. "It's these kids, huh? Aine only mentioned the girl when we talked, but I see you've got a boy too."

"Ahhh…" Iarumas muttered, looking up to the heavens as he struggled to figure out how he should respond.

After turning over hundreds of words in his head, Iarumas finally looked at Sezmar.

The fighter's helmeted head shook mercilessly, and he said, "I don't know what your situation is either. Can't help you here."

"I'll bet." Iarumas sighed. He adjusted the position of the bag he'd hauled back with him, then sighed again. "Drinks are on me, so help us out."

"Now you're talking," Sezmar replied. His face was hidden by his helmet, but he probably—no, *definitely* had a beaming smile on his face. That he could pull off this expression without seeming snide was a mark of the man's virtue.

With a call of, "It's time for some *drinks!*" to rile up the rest of his party, Sezmar turned back to Iarumas. "But really, though, how *is* it going? I'm interested."

"Well," Iarumas crossed his arms. Raraja gulped without realizing it. "They have potential. What they lack is experience."

"Oh, yeah? I see!"

Hearing that seemed to put Sezmar in an even better mood. He slapped Raraja on the back, the impact from his gauntleted hand making the boy stumble and blurt out, "Whoa?!"

"Good for you, young man. And little Miss Garbage too. That's high praise, coming from this guy."

Sezmar left Raraja to nearly topple over as he began vigorously mussing Garbage's hair. The girl protested with a "Yelp! Yelp!" as her curly, doglike hair ended up all frazzled.

Iarumas watched out of the corner of his eye as Garbage realized the futility of her resistance and settled down. He then shrugged and asked, "What's that supposed to mean?"

"Well, we'll talk about it over tonight's drinks," Sezmar replied. "Now, onward! To the tavern! Nothing beats a good stiff drink after an adventure!"

"Huh? Uh, wah…?!" Raraja babbled. Sezmar dragged him along by the arm, not letting him say a word otherwise, and Raraja nearly stumbled again. Although…yes, he *had* already been planning to accompany them based on how the conversation had gone so far. The firm grip of the gauntleted hand on Raraja's arm was painless but unshakable as an iron shackle.

Besides, with the All-Stars gathered around, there was no chance of him getting away.

"H-Hey, wait…!" Being led away like a prisoner, Raraja looked around for someone to save him, his eyes falling on the man in black.

His throat convulsed. The words spewed out, like he was speaking for the first time.

"Iarumas—Garbage!!!"

He got a response. Those clear blue eyes, like a spring of water, were focused on Raraja.

"Arf!"

Was she thanking him? Encouraging him? Telling him to give up? Or did it mean nothing at all?

Garbage trotted along behind Iarumas like a puppy following her master. As for Iarumas, he just shrugged and then continued forward at a relaxed pace.

Neither seemed likely to save him.

Fine by me, Raraja thought. This wasn't so bad. It was miles better than being in that rotten clan.

"You better remember this!" he shouted vengefully, then smiled. "I'm Raraja!!!"

In the end, when they got a bishop at the tavern—High Priest Tuck—to appraise their haul, the treasure was all dirt cheap. That was only by the standards of dungeon loot, though. If they took it to other lands, they could sell it for plenty of money—while they might not be set for life, they could fool around for decades with the income.

Iarumas was as good as his word, and once he'd paid High Priest Tuck for his services, he divvied up the spoils equally.

But...Raraja never considered leaving town with his share. Instead, his thoughts were about the dungeon, Iarumas, Garbage, his comrades, and his client.

And so, satisfied in the conclusion that things would work out better for him next time, he decided it was time to go dive into the straw of the stables and rest.

At least...for the time being.

Chapter 3
Scale

"You seem happy."

"Do I look it?" When Aine responded to Iarumas's comment, she did, in fact, sound positively exuberant.

It happened one afternoon at the temple.

The sun broke through the leaden clouds, warm and comforting.

A lot of guys would be jealous of him, having a conversation with a beautiful silver-haired elf like Sister Ainikki on a day like this.

That is, if it weren't taking place in the morgue...where they stored the dead bodies of adventurers.

"You do seem to be in high spirits." Iarumas had no idea why. Not that he tried to understand it.

If she's in a good mood, that's good.

Iarumas was the kind of man who could let it pass without caring to inquire further. He had enough trouble managing his own emotions. If she was going to take care of hers on her own, then that was for the best.

"Yep," Aine replied, not letting his indifference hurt her feelings. "I never thought I'd see the day when you'd find companions of your own."

"Companions?" he echoed, cocking his head to the side. His eyes fell on the girl who was sitting on the floor. She gave him a resentful growl.

"Companions..." he murmured again, looking at Raraja, who was cursing as he rifled through the possessions of the dead.

Iarumas sighed. "I'd never thought of them that way."

"Well, yes, we're talking about how I see it, not you."

It's a matter of perspective, then? Iarumas mused. He let out a quiet "hmmm," not bothering to disagree with her.

Well, it was true enough that, while he didn't know how long they'd be together, they were all heading to the dungeon once again...

"In that case," Iarumas said quietly, "I suppose I'll be needing some things."

"I'll come with you."

"Hm?"

He'd been murmuring to himself, but Aine had responded cheerfully. Seeing that he didn't understand her meaning, she pointed at him and said, "You're going shopping, right?"

Well, yes, he was. Iarumas admitted that. He didn't have anything to gain by denying it.

"Then, let me ask you this," Aine continued, smiling. "What are you going to be looking for?"

"Well..." Iarumas looked at Garbage and Raraja.

Messy red hair. A scrawny frame. A crude collar. Clothes that were basically rags. And a broadsword.

Unkempt black hair. A grimy body. Patchwork armor. A dagger that barely qualified as a weapon.

Having sized both of them up, Iarumas murmured, "Weapons and armor...and then potions and scrolls."

Though, the stuff available in shops was only so good. Helmets, target shields. Chain mail or breastplate for armor. Weren't there gloves of copper as well? As for potions and scrolls, the shops didn't stock anything particularly great, but the items they sold were valuable for a party without many spellcasters.

After all, Iarumas couldn't cast a single healing spell.

The biggest issue was right in front of him—would the nun (who was waiting for him to pay his tithe to the temple) tolerate him splashing out for all that stuff?

"You're hopeless..." Sister Ainikki said, repeating her comment from the other day, but this time with a smile. "I thought that might be the case."

"Then, it won't do?"

"No, I'm afraid it won't do at all," Aine agreed, nodding. "You two," she called out to the boy and girl.

"Yap!" Garbage responded first, barking and then rushing over to Aine—or more likely, to Iarumas. When Aine reached out a slender hand to pet her curly red hair, the girl closed her eyes contentedly.

Raraja, who followed Garbage, was moving rather sluggishly. "Man, I'm beat…" He tossed a sack full of stuff down on the ground—it landed with a metallic rattle.

All of it was equipment from lost adventurers.

If a corpse was left lying in the dungeon long enough, regardless of the state it was in, it sometimes rose up again, having lost its will. Or, if someone was in the morgue long enough, it was determined that no one would come to resurrect them, and they would be buried.

Souls extinguished, their names removed from the register… These were the lost, ones who could not even be turned to ashes.

When he had first learned about it, Raraja had seemed awfully panicked about something—but that was in the past now. Exhausted as he was, he didn't have the time to be concerned about others.

This had all started when the three of them had returned to the temple carrying corpses. Aine had greeted them with a smile and a request: "I'm going through some items—articles of the deceased that no one will come to collect—and then disposing of them. Could I ask you to help?"

When she mentioned that she would pay them for their time, Raraja had carelessly exclaimed, "You mean it?!" with a big smile on his face.

It was a given that labor should be compensated—the harsher the task, the greater the payment. And there were a *large* number of bodies… all of whom had died on the battlefield.

Collecting their equipment might have sounded simple, but it was difficult work to remove a helmet when it'd been broken, bent, crushed, melted, and then fused to a corpse.

Seriously, though…what killed these guys?

Raraja got a cold feeling in the bottom of his stomach when he tried to imagine it. On top of that, prying out the bits that were embedded in

93

dead flesh made his fingers ache. Even if they used tools like nippers, metal clippers, saws, and metal files, it was still hard work. And then, once they had pried the items free, they had to sort and categorize it all:

Things they could use, and things they couldn't. Things that could be sold, and things that couldn't.

Yes, that's right—some of these items would be sold. If they weren't going to be buried with the body, then most of them would be disposed of by the temple.

Basically, that's the temple's cut.

Iarumas didn't think it was especially greedy, but he couldn't blame anyone who criticized them for it.

"It was good training, wasn't it?" Aine said with a smile.

Raraja simply groaned, unable to say anything.

As she looked at the expressions on Garbage and Raraja's faces, Aine's smile softened more and more. "I don't think I can leave this to you..." the beautiful, silver-haired elf said, glancing at Iarumas. "So, I'll do you the favor of coming along."

§

To be more precise, she offered to pay them extra for carrying the arms and equipment to where they would be sold.

In for a penny, in for a pound. Raraja gritted his teeth as he strained under the heavy burden on his back.

"Dammit... You're really gonna pay us for this, right?!"

"I promised I would, so of course I will."

In the afternoon, Scale had an awfully relaxed, languid vibe to it. Most of the adventurers would have left for the dungeon in the morning, and the ones lingering behind were taking a break from work, so a calm atmosphere was only to be expected.

Still, that didn't mean the town was any less noisy. It was just that non-adventurers were making the noise instead. These people had gathered around to get their hands on the treasures that adventurers brought back, or to make some coin by offering services.

"Sell your unneeded arms and equipment here! We'll give you a quote for free if you're an adventurer!"

"If you've found an accessory, this is the place! We'll buy them off you at a high price!"

"Wanna play for a long time? How about a torch holder?! Unlike in the dungeon, you'll feel safe at night with one of these!"

"Western wine and northern mead! We deal in fine alcoholic beverages from all corners!"

"If you want to receive lessons on love from a Goddess, we can arrange them for you right away!"

"You can add an extra for just one silver!"

Just walking down the street, there were all sorts of voices echoing as businesses tried to call in customers. It was a chaotic mess, but all in service of giving adventurers a place to refresh themselves. One had to expect it would turn out like this.

Sister Ainikki walked along elegantly, letting no distaste for the state of things show on her face. Maybe that was why no one turned a curious eye toward Iarumas, though he was right next to her. Did they just not realize it was Iarumas because he was with a redheaded girl, a thief boy, and a nun?

Or maybe...they had mistaken Sister Ainikki for one of the *ladies of the night*?

That'd be a sacrilegious mistake if ever there was one...

Raraja had heard rumors of such women plying their trade in the shadows at night, by the graveyard or the temple. And the silver-haired woman walking in front of him sure was beautiful, with a healthy amount of meat on her bones. You didn't see her type back in his hometown...

"Is something the matter?" asked Aine.

"I-It's nothing..."

Whatever the reason for their indifference to Iarumas, all Raraja could do was focus on carrying the goods.

"So..." As if to banish his indecent thoughts, Raraja again asked, "You're *really* gonna buy us swords and stuff?"

"That will be for Iarumas-sama to decide," Aine answered with a chuckle, almost like she'd seen right through Raraja. "I'll just be sharing my opinion."

"Well, it would be good to get you a proper set of equipment," Iarumas said with an absentminded nod.

Raraja wasn't paying attention, though. Instead, he was imagining himself swinging around a greatsword. Not that he knew how to wield a sword properly...

In reality, the moves he fantasized about executing belonged to the girl trotting along ahead of him.

"Arf?" Garbage turned to stare at him as if she were asking, *"What do you want?"*

"It's nothing," Raraja replied.

The girl whipped back around, looking ahead once more. She scowled and shook her head at the noise, unable to understand anything the shop touts were shouting.

On the other hand, the scent of fried meat wafting from one of the food stalls got her sniffing with great interest.

"Blech..." Raraja frowned. "I'm amazed you still have an appetite..."

"Yap?"

They *had* just finished seeing all those dead bodies...even if she'd been looking less closely than Raraja had to. Given the blank look on her face, the experience must not have affected Garbage at all.

Noticing that she was getting ready to rush off toward the meat, an unornamented black gauntlet caught her by her red hair.

"We'll eat later," Iarumas told her.

Garbage let out a disappointed "Woof..." but didn't say anything more than that. She didn't resist and then obediently trotted after him, so they were probably getting along fine.

Even so...

Yeah, I don't get their relationship.

After concluding that, Raraja adjusted the position of the pack on his back, then followed the others without complaint. A little errand like this was no big deal compared to what his old clan had put him through. Besides, when it was done, he'd get money and equipment, so...

I'd be stupid to argue!

Could Raraja notice the difference in himself now that he had returned from the dungeon a number of times? He was carrying a load of equipment so heavy that no normal person could possibly bear it, and yet, his steps weren't shaky at all. Yes, he felt the weight of it biting into his shoulders, but it wasn't tiring him out in any other way.

Even if he had noticed, that on its own probably wouldn't be enough to make Raraja lose himself. His eyes were focused straight ahead of him on just one thing.

Garbage was trotting along in her carefree manner. On her back—a massive broadsword.

That's why, when Aine noticed and said, "Oh, dear," with a smile, it didn't even faze him.

Raraja just kept walking in silence, absorbed in his fantasies.

§

Eventually, they headed off the road, and Iarumas came to a stop in front of a sign.

"My, my…" Sister Ainikki's eyes twinkled.

"Hm," Garbage uttered, cocking her head to one side.

Raraja adjusted his pack, asking, "Here?" as he looked up at the sign.

It bore an image of a sword and shield, and beside them, the gently curled tail of a cat.

Catlob's Trading Post.

Was it a weapon shop? Raraja set his pack on the ground with a rattle as he peered at the sign.

"This the place?" he asked. "Hey, is something wrong?"

"Ahh. No…" Iarumas murmured, shaking his head. "It's just…every time I see it, I think the name seems familiar."

"Maybe you used to come here regularly?" Aine suggested.

"It's probably just the name I recognize."

"Still, that's a good thing." After all, she could easily count the number of times this man had shown an interest in something other than exploring the dungeon.

The more leads he can find to remember his past, the better.

Sister Ainikki's thin ears swayed with delight as she nodded. "If you manage to remember the past, maybe you'll stop being so obsessed with exploring the dungeon."

Iarumas smiled and opened the door. "That won't be happening." Garbage trotted behind him as he went through it.

When the girl turned back with an "Arf," Aine sighed, reaching for the door, and…

"Hm?" Noticing a strange look on Raraja's face, she stopped and turned to look at him. "Is something the matter?"

"No," Raraja murmured, the same as Iarumas had, then frowned despite himself. "What did you mean, *the past*…?"

He was hesitant to ask the question. He didn't think he should go digging into an adventurer's past. Raraja had his own examples of that. The stuff with his village. With the clan. With that girl. He wouldn't have wanted to talk about those things if anyone asked—but still, it bugged him.

The mystery man who dressed all in black… Raraja couldn't decide if he was a mage or a fighter…or what he was…

If he could get some insight into that guy, he wanted it…and could anyone really blame him?

Aine didn't really hesitate at the question. She stood at the door to the shop, glancing inside. "He doesn't remember anything from before he was resurrected, you know?"

"Huh…?" Raraja blurted out without meaning to. He hadn't known Sister Ainikki long, but he could already tell that he didn't need to doubt her when she told him something.

Even so, his incredulity had leaked out into his voice.

"I know it must be difficult to believe," Aine murmured with a chuckle deep in her throat. Her eyes were on the man who was already inside the shop. "I've heard that such things can happen when a person has their level drained by a succubus…"

A succubus, huh?

Raraja obviously hadn't ever encountered such a horrifying monster. Being a man, he kind of wanted to…but also as a man, he didn't want to let that fact be known.

"Succubus or not, I can't imagine him falling for a woman."

"You have a point there."

No, he doesn't seem like the type to be tricked by a succubus, Aine thought with a sigh. Besides, if he'd been sucked to death by a succubus, then it wouldn't have been possible to resurrect him. That death meant the complete loss of one's soul—Iarumas wouldn't be here if that was what'd happened to him.

Aine shook her head, her shimmering silver hair swaying with it. "Well, let's go in. I'm certain we'll find good equipment for you here."

Raraja followed her, his heart racing with excitement. Though it wasn't clear whether that was because of her smile...or the weapons.

§

"Look! Isn't it wonderful?!"

Sister Ainikki smiled broadly, holding an item close to the breast of her habit. If this had been happening at a normal shop—one for, say, apparel—a lot of guys would have been charmed to see the nun like this.

But this was an arms and armor shop, what she was hugging was a greatsword, and the man doing the looking was Iarumas.

With one cursory glance at the sword pressed between her breasts, he simply commented, "It might be good for Garbage."

The selection was overwhelming.

The moment Raraja set foot inside the store, he was struck dumb by the imposing shelves all around him. They were packed tight with more equipment than he'd ever seen in his life: swords, shields, armor, helms, staves, hammers, et cetera. There did seem to be a lack of bows or pole-arms like spears... Was it because the demand was highest for weapons that people could swing around in the dungeon?

It was strange—even the weapons that must've been sitting in the shop for a long time didn't have so much as a speck of dust on them.

This place is bigger than I thought... But it also feels cramped.

That was what crossed Raraja's mind as he took in the overwhelming selection on the shelves surrounding him. A huge amount of arms and armor were stocked, but that wasn't the only reason for the overpowering impression. The sword Aine was hugging emitted a pale blue light inside the dimly lit shop. *A magic weapon.* Glancing around, Raraja gulped as he saw more of them scattered here and there, each wrapped in a glimmer of its own.

And even if this place didn't have the legendary Lord's Garb in stock...

They might have elven chain mail.

The magic weapons all emitted a menacing aura that hung heavy in the air around Raraja.

"We'll be wanting a Mage Masher, I think..." murmured Iarumas.

"Oh? I'm more partial to the Blade Cusinart, myself."

The blasé way Iarumas and Aine talked (while Garbage watched them out of boredom, not listening to a word) was surreal. The atmosphere that filled this shop—Catlob's Trading Post—made Raraja feel strange.

"Customers?"

And that's why, though Garbage raised her head at the sudden question, Raraja couldn't move.

The voice was small, or perhaps thin, yet it projected mysteriously across the shop—a strange and beautiful sound. But its charm wasn't that of a musical instrument.

No, it was like the sharp edge of a well-honed dagger.

Raraja shuddered as he looked into the darkness of the shop, peering behind the register. He saw nothing but shadows...until, slowly, one shadow moved.

"Huh...?!" Raraja uttered in surprise.

"I smell the scent of the north sea...that land locked in eternal cold," said the voice. "Sister Ainikki."

"It's been a while."

After a moment, Raraja perceived that the shadow belonged to an elven man with cold-looking skin. There was no telling his age, as was always the case with elves. It was like guessing the age of an old tree. The man ignored Raraja, putting his hands together in a strange but respectful gesture as he faced Aine with a subtle bow of his head.

Then, slowly turning...

"Ah, the smell of old ashes. Iarumas. I hadn't expected you to still be alive."

"Well, I'm not dead, at least," Iarumas replied with the slightest of nods. "When I see you after being in this shop, it feels wrong somehow."

"It's a work name. I can't help that."

After listening to this exchange, Raraja finally figured out who the old elf must be.

The shopmaster—Catlob.

An elf, running an arms and armor shop? To Raraja's mind, that seemed more like a job for a dwarf...

"And I detect the sparkle of a honed diamond...while the other is still in the rough... Or perhaps, still coal." Snorting, Catlob looked at Raraja. "Rookies."

"Uh, sure..."

"Arf!"

Garbage barked like normal, unfazed by this assessment, while Raraja averted his eyes awkwardly.

Iarumas looked on indifferently. How unreliable. Aine nodded. That, at least, was a relief.

"W-We're h-here to sell," Raraja stammered, trying his hardest to speak. He then hurriedly added, "For the temple." Having said that, the boy set his heavy bag on the counter with a clatter.

Catlob groped blindly at the items in the bag, appraising them, but he moved so smoothly that it felt wrong to describe his motions that way.

His eyes...

Raraja shuddered as he realized that the man couldn't see. It felt like he could. But the reality was that the old elf's eyes weren't functioning.

Regardless, Catlob's sightless pupils pierced through Raraja's chest all the way to his heart.

"Many of these are damaged."

"Urkh..." Raraja gulped. "Not my fault. I had to tear them off..."

"It's because you bent the armor."

"Well, how else was I supposed to get them off?"

"Grind down the corpses."

"Blech..." As Raraja imagined the unpleasant scene, he let out a groan of disgust that bordered on a scream. He'd only *just* finished looking at all those monster-mauled cadavers.

However, *seeing* Raraja's distress, Catlob extended a hand to the boy. He had mysterious palms, possessing both un-elven coarseness and elven delicacy.

"You're a thief," he stated. "Get out your tools."

"T-Tools…?"

"Your *lock picking* tools. You're not about to tell me you don't have any."

Raraja did as the man said.

Garbage, Iarumas, and even Aine watched him with smiles. That embarrassed Raraja, but he knew it would be too childish to object. He'd kept these tools on his person at all times so that he could run away from Iarumas whenever he needed to.

Once he'd laid them out on the counter, Catlob needed only to touch them for the briefest of moments before he began openly scowling.

"What are these? Turds?"

"Oh, shut up," Raraja grumbled. "I've got all I need, don't I?"

"Did you make them yourself?"

"That a problem?"

"It is, yes."

These awkward, ill-made tools had been put together by Raraja out of a desperate need. There was no way someone in his situation wouldn't be upset at the disparaging remarks about his handiwork, but…

"Make some time and show your face around here," said Catlob. "I may be able to set you up with something a little more decent."

There was a silent, implied, *If you're not a total idiot,* that made Raraja fall into a resolute silence. He did not, however, decline the offer, because he was painfully aware of his own immaturity. Raraja needed to be able to survive on his own. That being the case, he wasn't going to turn down whatever help he *could* get from others.

Raraja knew he was weak, far too weak to be brushing off the assistance as unneeded and unwelcome.

Without another word to the boy, Catlob turned to Aine. "Payment will be made to the temple after the appraisal."

"Yes, that will be fine."

Catlob continued talking business with her. Raraja gave Iarumas a questioning look, and in response…

"Do as you like," Iarumas said. "Everyone should be free to raise their level however they see fit."

Permission? Uh, not that Raraja was Iarumas's subordinate or anything. This wasn't like his time in the clan. That's why Raraja let the man off with a petulant, "Oh, yeah?"

His eyes then went to the redheaded girl, who was just standing there with nothing to do, as always. Her frighteningly clear eyes looked back at him as if to say, *"Can I help you?"*

"Arf?"

"Must be nice for you, having it so easy…" Raraja muttered.

A girl who never spoke, who had been treated like leftover monster food, essentially a slave—a sullen man who, genuinely or not, claimed to have forgotten his past.

Compared to their situations, I don't have it so bad… was something Raraja never thought.

§

"What use does a thief have for weapons?"

Raraja's request for a sword had been mercilessly cut down by the shopkeeper.

"You don't need armor either."

Feeling dejected, Raraja said, "So you're telling me to die? Is that it…?"

"The thief's job is to deal with treasure chests," Catlob pointed out. "There's no point in you fighting before then."

"But," Iarumas interjected, stepping in to back Raraja up, "this kid's a front-liner."

"You—hurry up and get six people together," snipped Catlob in response.

Iarumas answered with a shrug before turning his impassive eyes toward the boy. "Choose whatever you like. I'm paying."

"You sure?"

"Even if I didn't, Aine would put it on my tab."

Raraja thought she probably would, given how things had gone so far. Aine's smile didn't fade at all when she heard Iarumas say that.

"Well then, I'll take this girl," Aine placed a hand on Garbage's shoulder, "and pick out some equipment for her."

"Yap?"

Aine ran her fingers lovingly through Garbage's red hair as the girl cocked her head to the side questioningly. The contact must have felt good, because Garbage's eyes narrowed happily.

"I'd like to get this collar off too...but forcibly breaking it would run the risk of hurting her."

Yeah—Garbage still had that crude, heavy collar hanging around her neck, glinting with its dark luster. Raraja wondered if it didn't feel heavy to her, but Garbage seemed to have accepted it as normal. If someone told Raraja she'd been born with it, he would believe them.

Sister Ainikki looked at Garbage and let out a pained sigh. "Well, come along—let's find you a lovely set of armor and a sword."

Garbage whined and gave a little snort, but did not resist. She followed Aine's lead into the back of the store.

That left Raraja, who glanced around awkwardly. No one gave him any further instructions.

"Erm..." Hesitantly, as if wandering through a dungeon, Raraja made his way toward the middle of the store.

Awesome.

His impression could be summed up in that one word.

Even though adventurers were up against monsters that seemed pulled from the age of myth, there wasn't much ingenuity in the selection of weapons available. In the end, it was all steel. Row upon row of it, tempered and tempered until it could be tempered no more. The steel shined radiantly, and the sight made Raraja gulp.

His own multipurpose knife was nothing in comparison. Neither were the swords wielded by the guys in his former clan.

"Were these...found in the dungeon?" Raraja murmured, not really hoping for an answer.

Catlob's low voice provided one nonetheless. "Some of them, yes. However, most were crafted by the hand of man. Few were 'discovered' there, in the truest sense of the word."

"Hm?"

"I'm referring, of course, to the category of items we would call... *legendary.*" There was something almost lyrical about the way Catlob spoke that last word.

Raraja couldn't imagine what he meant. Every one of the swords on the shelves here seemed legendary to him.

Not so to Catlob, apparently. The man let out a sigh, almost like he was gazing upon a mountain of trash. Then, he fell silent. Perhaps he thought he'd said too much.

Raraja reached out toward one of the knives on the shelf, unsheathing it. When he looked down at its blade...suddenly, the glint of the drawn sword he'd seen the other day came back to him. Images of a saber, like a black rod, and the man who carried it, wavered in Raraja's eyes.

"Iarumas."

"What?"

"Do you...want that sort of thing too?"

"I feel as though I've been seeking it," he murmured, shaking his head and seeming to reflect on the path he'd walked. That was an awfully vague answer, coming from Iarumas. "But, ultimately, it is a means. A means to an end."

"A means..."

"If I had one, it would be convenient, yes." Iarumas seemed to smile ever so slightly. "But if I don't, then so be it. There are other ways to proceed."

So wielding one wasn't essential. Raraja didn't understand how he could say that so dispassionately. *I guess that means his weapon's not the legendary whatsitsname, or whatever.* In that case, could Raraja get to the same level by just swinging around an ordinary knife?

The dagger in Raraja's hands felt unfamiliar as he played around with it some. It was a masterpiece unlike any he had touched in his life.

Catlob let out an audible sigh.

"This is why I don't like you."

At that moment, the door to the shop opened—a single customer entered.

§

"Huh…?"

Raraja recognized the customer, who wore a cloak covering them from the head down. Well, to be more precise, he recognized that *cloak*.

Strange, confused memories—blurred images, like water spilled over a picture.

Is it a mage?

"Ah!"

The instant Raraja made the connection to the man from the tavern a few days ago, a blade flashed from under that cloak.

Twin blades.

That was all Raraja understood. *Oh, crap.*

His body couldn't keep up with his conscious thoughts. No…that wasn't it. *My conscious thoughts can't keep up with my body.*

Just as he thought the blade had cut him, Raraja realized that he had, in fact, leaned back to dodge.

"Wuh, uh, wha, ahh?!"

I dodged that…?! He was more shocked by his body's reaction than by the surprise attack itself. It seemed that the thick stench of death in the dungeon had been remaking Raraja's body without him realizing it—not the physical structure of his flesh, but his spirit and concentration (HP). Now, even if Raraja didn't consciously notice incoming danger, his body would sense and avoid his impending death.

The attacker with the twin blades seemed just as shocked. Raraja sensed the man's eyes widening deep inside his cloak.

"Ow?!"

But that was all. Now that his mind had caught up to his body, he lost control of his limbs and fell over clumsily. Flat on his back, Raraja saw the ceiling.

Two blades streaked down toward him.

Death.

"Ruff!!!"

But Garbage was faster. The girl bounded over Raraja, barking—she loosed the broadsword from her back and swung it in one clean motion.

He's human.

That stupid thought flashed through Raraja's brain. Yes, they were facing a human—not a monster. It felt wrong, and that was what had made Raraja trip.

But Garbage moved with practiced finesse.

In mute shock, the man met her attack with his twin blades, eyes widening in yet more surprise. Metal screeched against metal as the two swords shattered—a powerful blow that belied the girl's slim arms.

Normally, the man would have been bisected from the head down, but his two curved swords held out just long enough to let him survive... like he was walking on thin ice.

"Eek?!"

An instant later, as her broadsword impacted the floor, Garbage let out a yelp, covering her face and doubling over backward.

Blow darts!

Another unconscious assessment had flashed across Raraja's mind before he could actively analyze the situation. The second the blow darts had appeared, he'd been aware of them.

Dammit! What the hell...?! He couldn't keep up with the gap between his conscious mind and his body. His muscles, nerves, eyes—they were all reacting too fast. It left his heart scrambling to keep up, and he felt frustrated and confused as his body did its own thing.

This internal discord was what kept him from being able to react properly.

"Waah?! Waah...!"

As it turns out, Garbage couldn't act either. Though, in her case, the needles sticking out of her face were at fault. She was shaking her head vigorously, trying to dislodge them, but the thin, silver darts weren't going to come out so easily.

"Hey, don't touch that," Catlob warned in a level voice.

That was when Raraja finally noticed what their attacker was doing. Having lost his weapon, he'd selected a new one from the racks. A ringing sound came from the scabbard as he drew this new blade—a strange weapon wreathed in a demonic purple haze emerged from the sheath.

And that wasn't all—no.

As he stood in silence, the eyes of the assassin, which had previously harbored a sharp, murderous glint, suddenly grew dull. His relaxed posture and the way he now held his sword… It was a complete departure from not just his earlier fighting stance, but from everything else about him.

However, he wasn't in a daze. His unfocused eyes were turned toward Raraja.

There was only one probable cause.

"A…A demon sword…?!" Raraja stammered. The boy rose shakily to his feet, somehow managing to settle into a fighting posture with the dagger he held.

Garbage was still thrashing around on the floor. At the moment, it didn't look like Raraja would be able to rely on her skills, even if he'd wanted to. But he didn't. Something small inside his chest wouldn't allow it.

However, he had no qualms about requesting aid from the rest of the room. "Hey, do something!" Raraja shouted.

"What is that, um…dull sword?" Iarumas asked.

Why is the man most capable of helping just watching with his arms crossed?

The shopkeeper, observing with unseeing eyes, was no better. When he answered, his tone was full of delight. "It's the Sword of Swisher. That one's a part of my personal collection, not for sale. It's an excellent sword, isn't it? The work of ancient magic and smithing techniques. The curse… is but a minor detail."

"A broadsword, huh?" Iarumas smiled. "What an accursed name."

"What kind of nonsense are you—?!"

—*talking about.* That's how Raraja would have finished his sentence…but he didn't get the chance. Suddenly, the assassin came at him, attacking like a puppet controlled by strings.

"Wh-Whoa?!" One of Raraja's arms reflexively shot up, parrying the

Sword of Swisher with the dagger. Sparks flew inside the dark shop. Raraja stumbled a couple of steps, but Garbage was cowering on the floor right behind him. The boy gritted his teeth, holding his ground so he wouldn't squash her, then surged forward.

"Grah!!!"

It was a desperate attack. But the dagger in his hand really seemed to have settled into his palm just right.

Wow... This is...

Awesome!

It was exhilarating, moving, empowering. He, the lowest of the low, was managing to trade blows against a demon sword. This battle felt totally different from when he'd faced the dragon. That time, it had been a question of whether or not he could survive in the face of an overwhelming monster.

In this case, the stakes—life or death—were similar.

Once, twice, and again. Raraja desperately parried the wild swings of the sword's new puppet. It took everything he had to protect himself. His hand was going numb. Honestly, he had no confidence that he could win this, but...

May...be.

Perhaps he *could* win. He was putting up a good fight. That fact made him feel light-headed.

Yes—even though his thoughts still hadn't caught up with the reflexive actions of his body, his mind was getting giddy all on its own.

"Ah...?!"

Bwoosh. He'd gotten greedy, offensively swinging out his blade, but it'd sliced through the air with more momentum than he'd expected.

Oh, crap.

He sensed it instinctively. The fatal opening. The incoming blade.

Death.

He'd made just one mistake, but it had been fatal...

"Hahhhh...!"

The sudden battle cry that rang out sounded so dignified that it actually came across as kind of cute.

Thud! Raraja felt the floor shake. He saw a colored wind blow past him—a silver and black figure leaped forward, leaving a smattering of smoking footprints on the old wooden floor.

The figure had the general shape of Sister Ainikki…but with a greatsword pulled taut to strike.

"Yahhhh!!!"

She wound back all the way and then unleashed like a spring mechanism. Her sword kicked up a gust of wind, the blade leaving a single trail behind it as it arced through the air. There was no sound, but Raraja thought he saw a flash of light.

Silence from everyone in the room. And then…

Nothing happened.

The man's arms simply slumped, almost like his strings had been cut.

She…missed?

Even Raraja, who'd gotten a front-row seat to the action, assumed that. However, an instant later, the man's knees gave out, and—*splash!*—a dark red flower bloomed.

His head flew off.

Then, his body slumped over sideways. The head that had once sat atop his shoulders now spun as it bounced across the floor. Once the head was gone, the body it left behind gushed blood from the gaping wound.

Oh, so this is what it means when they talk about it raining blood… thought Raraja.

"May you have a good death under the protection of God…" prayed Aine as she bathed in the falling drops of ichor. "Whew." She exhaled, then spun around.

"Hey now, Iarumas-sama!"

Whoosh! Her sword whipped right past Raraja's nose to point directly at the man in black.

"That wasn't very noble of you! Just watching like that…"

Iarumas pushed aside the tip of the blood-drenched sword with some irritation, then shrugged his shoulders. "I thought he'd manage without my intervention." No panic, no surprise. No concern or relief either. He spoke as if he was only stating the facts. "Simply gaining experience in the dungeon isn't enough to say you've raised your level."

Taking a break. Resting in town. That was the important thing, Iarumas explained dispassionately. Then, he continued, saying, "It was the same way for me… Probably."

When Iarumas stepped forward to clap Raraja lightly on the shoulder, his boots made a squelching sound in a puddle of blood. He then crouched next to Garbage, staining his knees red as he peered at her face.

"I'm pulling them out. Don't move."

She just whined in response. There was a jingle as the silver needles scattered across the floor. Though the darts were thin and sharp, they fortunately hadn't gone in all that deep.

With the needles pulled out of her eyelids, Garbage hesitantly opened her blue eyes.

"Arf!"

Once he'd seen her eyes—like two deep pools of clear water—blink a few times, Raraja let out a sigh of relief. Maybe…he'd been trying not to notice them too much before now.

"Ah, jeez…" Sister Ainikki let out a resigned sigh, seemingly unconcerned by the blood splatter. Then, she noticed the disbelief on Raraja's face. "Oh," she murmured, looking around before adding, "gosh." Her cheeks flushed red—the color of roses, not blood—and she began fidgeting awkwardly. "I'm sorry. Look at what I've done."

Thoroughly embarrassed, she held out the greatsword like it was a fashionable piece of clothing and asked, "Will you be buying this?"

§

Having added one more two-handed sword to the list than they'd originally planned, their shopping trip ended without further incident.

It was now evening, and Raraja trudged down the main street in Scale, a weary look on his face.

"This wasn't worth it…" he muttered.

Beside him walked a thoroughly apologetic Aine. "I'm terribly sorry…" she said. Her silver hair swayed in the golden light of sunset as she bowed her head.

When she was that sincere, it made Raraja feel awkward. "Nah," he curtly told her. "It's no big deal—I'm used to being an errand boy."

In the end, he'd had to carry the body.

"I won't ask you to clean up the blood, but don't leave a headless body lying in the middle of my store. It's your job, isn't it?"

After things had wound down, it'd been decided that they would follow Catlob's eminently reasonable suggestion and bring the man's body back to the temple.

That said, Iarumas needed to buy equipment for Raraja and Garbage, so he couldn't leave right then. Aine had offered to do it, but they couldn't make her haul the corpse while she was still covered in blood. And, as for having Garbage carry it...well, there were all sorts of worries that came with that idea.

That only left Raraja.

Reluctance, resignation, a sense of duty. He took on the task, all the while feeling something that didn't neatly fit into any of those categories.

If all I need to do is haul a corpse for them, then it's still better than what the clan had me doing. Taking a corpse to the temple rather than leaving it behind to rot in the dungeon... This felt better to Raraja, if only a little. Though, that said, this particular corpse wasn't exactly an adventurer who'd fallen in the dungeon.

Overall, Raraja was fine with all of it—he had no issues finding his way back to the temple, and no problem expending his time and stamina along the way.

No, the biggest issue was...

"I told the other priests that Iarumas chopped up a shoplifter."

"I'm really sorry..." Aine replied.

Raraja couldn't possibly tell the temple that one of their own nuns had swung around a greatsword and lopped the guy's head off.

It might've been a bit of a stretch to say that Raraja lied for her because of his morals... Rather, he didn't want to hurt the reputation of someone who'd helped him.

Well, I don't really mind if it's Iarumas...

And so, that's how he'd ended up explaining this made-up story to the temple priests at length.

"I've never had such an earnest, face-to-face conversation with priests in my entire life..."

"Arf?"

Trotting along the road with them, Garbage snorted dubiously at the way Raraja was acting. What an interest she took in her fellow humans. By contrast, Iarumas, who was walking ahead of them, didn't so much as look back.

Regardless, Raraja was mentally and physically exhausted. He also didn't have the will or pride to try and hide it, which showed a lack of maturity on his part.

"Man, I'm tired..." As far as he was concerned, he wasn't complaining, just grumbling, but it made Aine feel awkward. While Raraja had run off to the temple, she'd cleaned herself up. He thought she must've used a spell of some sort—after all, if all she had done was change her clothes, that wouldn't have gotten the caked blood off her cheeks and out of her hair. In addition, even though they hadn't put down sawdust or anything, the blood puddles on the shop floor had completely vanished.

Or...maybe Catlob's Trading Post was just set up to handle that kind of thing...

Anyway, that's enough of a digression.

At any rate, Scale was noisy in the early evening, more so than it had been during the day. The parties who'd made it back from the dungeon were out celebrating their victorious return, using the money they'd earned adventuring.

It wasn't unusual to see groups walking around covered in blood—but a solitary nun? That would've stood out in a bad way. If she were still stained in crimson, Sister Aine would have shrunken into herself, smaller than a mouse. Or perhaps her faith, which did not dread death, would have allowed her to walk the streets, head held high.

I wouldn't like that.

Raraja figured she ought to leave that shtick to Iarumas and Garbage.

"O-Oh, I know...!" Aine suddenly clapped her hands together, drawing the group's attention in a way that came across as kind of forced.

They had come to stop right in the middle of the main road, so the flow of people quickly cut the group in two. Aine smiled, ignoring the passersby who eyed them dubiously. "As thanks for your help earlier, I'll treat you at the tavern tonight!" she exclaimed. "Yes, that sounds good!"

"Yap?"

"I know, right?!" Aine replied cheerily.

"Seriously?" asked Raraja.

"Yes, quite!"

Garbage didn't know what the nun was talking about, and Raraja was surprised, but Sister Ainikki wouldn't let either of them escape.

Oh well. It wasn't like Raraja had any intention of running off on her. He was hungry, his throat was parched, his feet ached, and his whole body felt heavy. Though he hadn't noticed it, Raraja's concentration (HP) had been run down to almost nothing, and not just by the battle in the weapon shop—there were lots of ways to exhaust yourself that didn't involve fighting.

With Raraja and Garbage in agreement about Aine's offer, that meant the only potential remaining problem was the person at the front of the group—the man in black.

"The tavern, huh?" Iarumas said, letting out a sigh. "I won't be getting my hopes up…"

Raraja didn't understand what Iarumas meant by that mumbled response. But apparently, Aine did. She leveled a finger at Iarumas with a mixture of astonishment, kindness, and irritation.

"The tavern is for more than just gathering party members, you know?"

"What else is it for, then?"

"For food and drink. It's a place that's essential for enjoying all life has to offer."

"You know, from what I've seen—" Raraja began, deciding to mercilessly stab Iarumas in the back. *Consider this payback for sitting back and watching me almost get killed.* "—all this guy ever eats is gruel."

"Oh, my goodness…!" With an expression of exasperation, Aine, who was beautiful even with her attractive eyebrows arched, came to a stop in front of a drinking establishment.

The sign, which bore the name of an old god, read, "Durga's Tavern."

§

"Whoa...?!"

The moment they came through the door, the roar of noise hit them like dragon's breath. This mass of information smacked into Raraja so hard that it nearly bowled him over.

All around him, there was talk of what appeared on which floor of the dungeon. Expensive pipe-weed. Greasy cooking. Booze. The clinking of gold coins. Laughter. Tears.

Adventurers celebrated coming back alive, boasted about making two hundred gold coins, and mourned the loss of a party member's soul. This crowd enriched themselves in the dungeon, or enriched the dungeon with themselves.

Durga's Tavern was the biggest adventurer's inn in all of Scale—Raraja had learned that the other day. But just because it was his second time here didn't mean he was used to the place. Though, yes, he had stayed at an inn, his lodging had always been in the stables. He'd never had anything to do with the tavern in the early evening when it was at its busiest—not before, and not now.

"Come on, eat your fill," urged Aine. "Don't hold back on my account. This is important for adventurers like you!" She led the way into the tavern, swimming through the crowd like she was parting the sea for her companions.

Iarumas trailed her like a shadow, while Raraja and Garbage looked like they were going to get caught in the crush of people. Once they followed the two adults to a round table, Raraja slumped into a seat, exhausted.

Finally, I can sit...

Mysteriously, he'd felt fine while standing, but the day's fatigue seemed to strike him all at once now that he was sitting.

And…the day wasn't over yet.

Sitting next to Garbage, who was looking small and quiet, Raraja clung desperately to the table.

"Would you like some meat, Garbage-san?" Aine asked.

"Yap!"

Where does all her energy come from? Even if Garbage couldn't understand Aine's words, the emotion in them (or something like that) still got across to the girl.

Raraja turned a dubious eye toward Garbage as she barked cheerfully. Now that she and Aine were distracted, there was only one person left to talk to…

"What about you?" Iarumas asked.

"I'll…eat." Raraja replied to the gloomy, inscrutable man.

Iarumas nodded, then called over one of the waitstaff. He placed their order, showing no particular emotion, then concluded with an indifferent "And I'll have the gruel."

"No, that won't do," Aine objected sharply. She rattled off an order which, if Raraja hadn't misheard, included a strong northern liquor and several other dishes. Then, throwing an arm around Iarumas's shoulders, she held him close to her chest, just like she'd done with the greatsword.

"I'm sorry, Raraja-san, but could you look after Garbage-chan?" Slowly, the elf's beautiful eyes turned to glare at Iarumas. "I need to have a word with Iarumas-sama."

"A sermon, huh?"

"Indeed!"

There was no time for objections. Raraja offered a silent prayer that Iarumas might rest in peace as he watched the two of them go off together. Though, a death that involved Sister Ainikki watching over his final moments couldn't be that terrible…

"Urkh…" Raraja scowled, suddenly recalling the weight of the corpse he had carried earlier. That man's life had been snuffed out in an instant…

Meat? Raraja didn't have the appetite for it now.

But…

"Sorry for the wait!"

"Arf!"

The server appeared, roughly setting down trays of food, and Garbage barked her approval of the meat—the cuts were sizzling away on top of a hot iron plate. It looked like Aine had really splurged on them.

"Yay!!!" Garbage shouted. If it weren't for the hot plate, she would've surely grabbed the meat with her hands to take a bite.

Instead, she used a knife and fork to cut and stab, pouncing on her meal with gusto.

I'm amazed she can eat... When he thought back to the disaster that had unfolded earlier, Raraja felt like someone had crushed his stomach in their fist.

He'd been sent flying before. Had nearly been killed too. But...

Trying to kill someone...

It might not have been the first time he'd *threatened* to kill someone...but it'd been the first time he'd genuinely tried to carry out the act. Killing a person wasn't like killing monsters. Even when he'd gone after Iarumas, he'd only meant to rough him up a bit, at most.

And yet, this girl... She hadn't hesitated to swing a broadsword at their attacker.

What kind of life has she led?

She had a crude, thin collar around her neck. Her intelligence was practically the same as a feral dog's. She spoke no words. The only thing she had...was a sword.

"Hm?"

Garbage's head shot up. Perhaps she'd reacted because Raraja was looking at her as he mulled things over. Her blue eyes—slightly dark, like a bottomless pool of clear water—stared piercingly back at him.

He gulped despite himself.

She chewed loudly in response.

Without having to think about it, he understood what she meant. "I'm gonna eat it..." he told her. "You can't have mine."

"Arf," she said, which seemed to mean, "*Oh, okay then.*" Garbage then snorted and returned to fighting with a thick piece of meat.

Raraja let out another sigh, taking his fork and knife in hand. If he didn't eat, it would feel like he'd lost...and that would really bother him. Besides, if he could just banish the man's corpse from his mind's eye, he'd be able to eat some quality meat. This wasn't a chance that came along often…

At least, up until now. He didn't know how things would be from here on out. That thought helped whet his appetite.

"All right!" With that settled, Raraja got ready to dig in, but then…

"Hey, kiddo! You're still alive, huh?!"

He was interrupted by a raucous shout and a hearty slap on the back.

§

"Ha ha ha ha, sorry, sorry!"

Raraja and Garbage were now seated at Sezmar's table—the All-Star's table. When he was with this bighearted free knight, Raraja could never respond with much more than a mumbled, "Right" or "Nah." This was their second meeting. It was great that they were friendly, but the six of them were in a league way above his own.

Yes, that's right—he was surrounded by all six of them today. He felt like he might die at any moment.

Garbage, who they'd also dragged along, was sitting across the table, munching away at her meat indifferently. Raraja couldn't believe it…

"You're always like this, Sezmar," complained Sarah. "Try to be nice to the rookies, would you?"

"You say that, but I know you're always acting like the know-it-all senior adventurer," countered Moradin.

"Hey, Prospero!" Sarah called out, turning to the mage. "Tell this rhea off for me!"

"For my part, I think you can be just as rude as Sezmar…" said Prospero.

"What'd you say…?!"

"I can't identify items with all this racket!" snapped High Priest Tuck. "Take a lesson from Hawk! You should all be more like Hawkwind!"

After all, *this* was how they acted…

The elven priest and the rhea thief were at one another's throats, while the mage declared neutrality and the dwarf got mad at all of them.

Every one of them was such a storied adventurer that Raraja and Garbage should have been beneath their notice.

Urghhhh...

Surrounded on all sides, Raraja wanted nothing more than to run away from them immediately. The eyes of the adventurer who hadn't been here the other day—a mysterious man clad all in black—affected him especially badly.

That man, Hawkwind, just sat in silence, tilting back his drink. The bowl in front of him, which had held gruel, was already empty, so he was just hanging around to be with his companions.

Yet, the way his eyes silently sized up Raraja...was incredibly disconcerting. The boy couldn't put his finger on it, but there was something about the man—something that reminded him of Iarumas.

He had that sort of strange look in his eyes...like he didn't see people as people.

Raraja silently gulped. No matter what he said, it would be dangerous to open his mouth—that was the sense he got.

"Um, err, uh..." Raraja looked around, avoiding eye contact as he searched for a topic that would get him out of there. A mound of valuable items sat on the table before them, and the dwarf was diligently inspecting the pile. This was his ticket.

"Tuck...-san."

"Just High Priest is fine." The kindly dwarven bishop gave a smile that looked to have been hewn from stone. "What is it, young'un?"

"It really helped us out when you appraised our stuff last time, but don't you ever...just get it assessed at the shop?" With this volume of treasure, it seemed like it would be more trouble than it was worth for the dwarf to do it all himself. Raraja had just been trying to change the topic, but it was also something he'd genuinely wondered about.

"At Catlob's place?" Tuck scowled. "He'd rip us off."

"The price he charges for item appraisal is the same amount he's willing to buy stuff for!" added Sarah.

"He only runs that shop to amuse himself," scoffed Prospero. "He doesn't care one whit about his customers."

With Sarah and Prospero chiming in, a mountain of complaints about Catlob soon rolled out. Apparently, he would buy cursed items at a high price...but if you asked him to break the curse, he would charge for the service and then keep the item.

That's funny...

Raraja cracked a smile. It was twitchy, but he forced himself to keep it up as he asked, "Is it because he wants to put them on display?"

"Isn't it so tasteless?" Sarah griped.

"He's got the legendary weapons...though, not any one in particular, seared into his memory," the rhea, Moradin, murmured with a secretive snicker. He started stuffing his pipe with pipe-weed, lit it with a trick that seemed almost like magic, and then, *poof,* began blowing smoke rings. He blew another thin wisp of smoke to thread the ring, then looked at Raraja. "Well, anyone who makes their way to this town has some goal in mind, big or small. It makes things easy to understand."

"Does that—"

—include Iarumas too?

The man in black had no memories. Was he searching for them? If so, then what had his former self been seeking?

Raraja had lapsed abruptly into silence. How did the rhea thief interpret it? Well, Moradin may have been trying to be a good senior to his less experienced colleague because he spoke in a serious tone, uncharacteristic of his race. Slowly, he explained things to Raraja.

"You've gotta watch out, kid," he warned. "Powerful magical items can drive you nuts even when they're just sitting there."

"That sounds especially meaningful coming from a rhea," said Raraja.

Moradin shrugged. "Tell me about it!"

High Priest Tuck turned his eyes, which gave off an impression of prudence, toward Raraja. "But magic weapons aren't what's dangerous— it's the hearts of their wielders that are truly terrifying."

"Their hearts?" Raraja repeated.

"Sure. Basically, a person might think, 'If it's me, then *I* can master it. I can get my hands on one. And once I have it, I'll do wonderful things.'"

"If it's me…" Raraja murmured.

Tuck nodded. "Precisely. As is, pride is already a sickness that invites death."

"High Priest, now *you're* acting like a know-it-all senior adventurer," Sarah said, cackling. The elf looked drunk—her ears had gone red. That's likely why the dwarf didn't bother taking her seriously.

I kind of get it.

Raraja descended into a sea of thought, cutting himself off from the boisterous adventurers he was sitting with. After all, he'd had his own experience just the other day—with the Demon's Stone—and it had ended badly…

Yet, despite losing the stone, he was still thinking, *If I could use it properly, it'd sure be convenient to have.*

Subtly, Raraja reached for the dagger on his hip, stroking the hilt. It wasn't a magic weapon, of course. But it was a masterpiece unlike any he could have imagined before now. Now that he had it…could he really claim that he wouldn't embarrass himself again like he had earlier?

Suddenly, a booming voice, as loud as when he'd been slapped on the back earlier, startled Raraja.

"If you play with weapons, your luck will drop."

"Whuh?!"

That infuriatingly cheerful voice and refreshing smile belonged to Sezmar, now with his helmet removed.

"I get how you feel though," he continued, "since you just got a new weapon. Why don't you think about something fun instead?"

"Uh, no, I wasn't…"

Nah, he's right. Raraja had just been warned that overconfidence was a disease…but optimism wasn't the same as overconfidence. He'd survived up until now. They'd bought him a new dagger today, and he had food in front of him.

It would be weird to get depressed. He ought to enjoy the moment. That's why…

"You don't look like you ventured into the dungeon," remarked Sezmar. "So where'd you get that?"

When asked the question, Raraja smirked—*I'll enjoy this too*—and told them all the tale.

"Well, you see, Sister Ainikki told Iarumas—"

§

Durga's Tavern went wild. People pounded their tables in amusement, glasses were raised, and adventurers laughed uproariously.

Raraja sat in the middle of it, astonished—but he looked a lot more cheerful now.

"Hey, is Aine-san *really* a nun?" he asked. After seeing her swing a greatsword around like that, he had a hard time believing it. Could it be? Was she actually a knight of the church, or paladin—a lord?

It was Sarah who answered (answered?) his question. "No comment. Now, let's talk about Iarumas! I'm already miffed that he's eating with Aine, but how could he leave a cute girl like this all alone?!"

At some point, she had wrapped her slender arms around Garbage.

The girl was scrawny and underfed once you took her broadsword away from her. Sitting on the elven priest's lap, she looked just like a little puppy.

"Hey, you agree, don't you, Garbage-chan?"

"Woof…"

The girl seemed rather put out by Sarah's fawning—it seemed that the display of affection only went one way.

As the elf rubbed cheeks with Garbage, Raraja easily ignored the blue eyes that peered at him resentfully. Even if he'd wanted to help her, Raraja didn't have anywhere near the courage it would take to defy even one of these six adventurers.

"You're so harsh on Iarumas," Sezmar said with a laugh. "He's not such a bad guy, you know?"

"That's *not* the problem here." Sarah vigorously petted Garbage—who was trying to eat meat—before irritably continuing, "You know different people see the dungeon differently, right?"

"What's Iarumas say he sees?"

"*Darkness and white lines,*" Sarah replied, looking at the rest of the group dubiously. "Can you believe that?"

"Nah, that can't be true. No way," Moradin waved his little hands dismissively. "That's gotta be bull."

"Ha ha ha! If you ask me, it sounds like a tasteful way of seeing things!" Tuck remarked.

"Iarumas is a mage, like myself," Prospero pointed out. "That being the case, he should be able to see things at a deeper level."

"Perhaps your skill is low, and you're just being led astray by illusions," joked the dwarf.

They all bantered back and forth, saying whatever they liked—Hawkwind alone was sullenly silent. No, not just him. Raraja was the same, not contributing anything either.

Everyone who comes to this town has some objective, big or small.

Was that true of Iarumas?

Raraja's question from earlier had come back to him.

Even now, after losing his memories, Iarumas ventured into the dungeon. Was it *because* he'd lost them?

Who is he? Where did he come from? And where is he going?

No, before all of that…

"Before all that…" The words leaked from Raraja's mouth unbidden, seeming to spill out naturally. "It's questionable whether Iarumas is even his real name…"

"Yeah, it's probably an alias." That answer, which came so easily, was provided by Moradin, who was sucking on his pipe.

"An alias?"

"Of course. I'm hiding my name too. And so is Mr. Catlob." Moradin snickered teasingly, and his laugh seemed to ask, *Did that guy look like he was cute enough to be a Catlob?*

"We're adventurers," the rhea continued. "No one's gonna mind what we call ourselves—it can be whatever we want."

Raraja fidgeted awkwardly because he *was* using his real name.

This experienced rhea thief must have understood how Raraja felt. His tone softened a little—or so the boy thought, though it could have been his imagination. "Well, I figure that's better than giving yourself a work name or a nom de guerre just because you want one."

Raraja breathed a sigh of relief—he'd managed to get the All-Stars talking. Maybe it was because of all the alcohol he'd drunk throughout the conversation...despite being too tense to taste it. Not that it mattered to him either way. What Raraja had wanted, from the bottom of his heart, was courage.

"So, the names... What about you guys?" Raraja asked.

"Mine's real," Sezmar said with a laugh. "Comes from a hero from long ago."

"Mages hide their true names."

"Not me," Sarah said, acting as if she'd found Prospero's answer boring. Then, with her nostrils flaring, she added, "If Garbage is her real name, I'll give her parents a thrashing."

"Meh..." Garbage was still in Sarah's lap, wrapped in an adoring hug. Had she given up on resisting? She seemed to have gone mostly limp while lazily piling meat into her mouth.

She shot glances at Raraja, still wordlessly crying for help, but he ignored them.

"Come to think of it—is 'Hawk' a work name too?" Sarah asked.

"Probably, right?" Tuck guessed. "I don't think he's ever told us."

When they asked him, "Hey, how about it?" Hawkwind just shrugged silently.

But even that was outside Raraja's thoughts.

For the rest of the night, Raraja didn't say anything.

§

And so, an extremely eventful day came to a close.

From corpse-looting in the temple to the day's end celebration at the tavern, Raraja had been at the mercy of the flow of events...which had now deposited him on the straw of the stables.

Aine had gone back to the temple; Iarumas had sought out his room, and Garbage had trotted off after him.

Raraja was now alone, his exhausted body sinking into the straw as he gazed absently up at the ceiling.

So...tired...

He'd been through way too much...just so much...from morning until night.

Hauling corpses, going to the weapon shop, being attacked by some kind of robber, buying the dagger, going to the tavern.

Some of it had gone well; some of it hadn't. He felt like *most* of it hadn't.

Y'know, that guy... The man in the tavern who'd hired Raraja—if you could call it that—had set him up as an assassin. The robber in Catlob's had been wearing an identical cloak, so the two men must've been part of the same group... Right?

There was no way to find out now—the robber was missing his head. And there was no way to resurrect him for free.

Still, though... Couldn't he have handled things better? Both the guy...and Raraja himself.

Sure, Raraja had been forced onto the defensive, but there was no way he should have gone for a big swing like that. If he'd been down in the dungeon...

No...

If Sister Ainikki hadn't been there, I'd be dead.

Her moves had been incredible. Garbage's too, even though she'd messed up. Raraja couldn't move anything like that.

And then...there was Iarumas. Raraja had caught a glimpse of his moves the other day, down in the dungeon...

He was incomparably quick. The All-Stars were probably just as fast.

Raraja *had* gotten faster, but the others were all on another level entirely.

Sure, you could say it's a difference in experience, and that'd be the end of it...

But the way Raraja used his body, the way he moved... It had to be a major factor. As long as he was still being jerked around by his own body, he'd never get anywhere.

At the very least, I need to get used to the way I am now...

Beyond the edge of the world… If Raraja was going to see what was out there, then he couldn't neglect the ground beneath his own feet. Because, unlike with his former clan, he was now in a position to build a solid foundation.

As he lay there peacefully, it all began coming together in his head…

Ah.

"It was the same way for me… Probably."

So that's how it was, huh? Raraja let out a sigh at the realization.

Yeah…it was Iarumas. The reason Raraja was alive. The reason he was now able to spend his days in ways he'd never imagined before. It was all unquestionably because of (not "thanks to"—he refused to admit that) the man in black.

But, at the same time, Raraja didn't know. He didn't know what Iarumas and Sister Ainikki had talked about, or what Garbage was thinking.

What's going on with all of them?

Aine and Garbage. The All-Stars. Iarumas.

Why did they come here? Where from? And where were they going?

What was he—Raraja—exactly? What could he become?

The boy thought it over sluggishly until his consciousness broke, and he sank into darkness.

He would awaken once more when the dawning sun cast its first light into the stables. When the morning came, all these thoughts would be long gone.

And the dungeon…would be waiting.

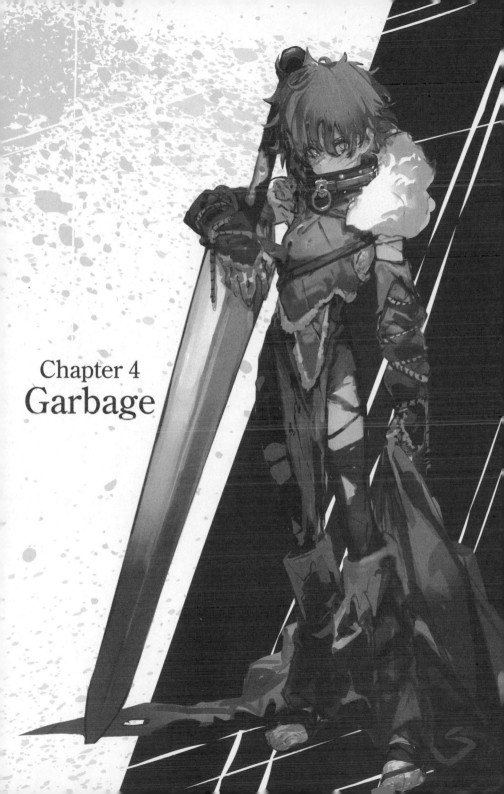

Chapter 4
Garbage

"Wiped out…"

All of this started because of that murmur in Durga's Tavern.

It was morning. The tavern was bustling, but not overcrowded—there were still seats available.

Iarumas, who was in the corner eating gruel, heard the sudden voice. He didn't look up, just kept silently spooning food into his mouth.

That day, Iarumas's party was taking a break. He, of course, was not fond of taking time off work. However, their group didn't include a priest, and without the aid of healing magic, their bodies needed time to recover naturally. As such, there were times when they had no choice but to spend several days at the inn.

It seemed like the distressed man had been aiming for that.

The man suddenly opened the doors to the tavern—as usual—and stumbled inside. He was unkempt, and if someone were to call him a "bushwhacker," well, he certainly looked the part. Perhaps he'd been drinking somewhere else before arriving at the tavern because he seemed unsteady on his feet.

In addition, the man was muttering to himself repeatedly.

"Wiped out…"

But so what? A party being wiped out wasn't so unusual. No one was going to stop and listen to him. Iarumas just scarfed down more gruel.

A party of adventurers getting wiped out in the dungeon wasn't even worth talking about. Especially if they weren't a famous group like Sezmar's All-Stars. There were too many small-time adventurers out there, all calling themselves the heroic band from some country or other.

Glancing around at the few empty seats available, the man picked out one right behind Iarumas and sat down. The heavy slumping sound caused Iarumas to raise an eyebrow ever so slightly.

"The third floor…" mumbled the man. "Deep in the third floor… A hidden door… That's where, ahh…"

The man just kept talking as Iarumas packed away his gruel. Though he was supposedly muttering to no one in particular, he was going into awfully specific detail about how his party had been defeated.

The third floor. A hidden door no one else had discovered—a group of monsters behind it. A treasure chest. A trap…

"I'm the only one left… Just me… My comrades… They're still…" The man kept on going. Though he wasn't speaking to anyone in particular, the volume of his voice meant that his words still reached people's ears.

Eventually, satisfied that he'd said enough, the man slowly got up and staggered off. It wasn't clear where he was going, but he left the tavern, vanishing off into town.

No one paid attention to him—the same as when he'd appeared. That included Iarumas.

However, he could tell, even without looking, that the man had worn a cloak much like a mage's.

"Honestly." Iarumas dropped his spoon into his empty bowl and smiled. "Could it be any more blatant?"

§

"Would you cut it out?!"

"Arf!"

Garbage traipsed through the dungeon again today, heedless of the complaints coming from behind her.

This was an everyday occurrence.

Venture underground, broadsword in hand. Slay monsters. Find treasure chests. Open them.

Well, no—opening chests had strange results a lot of the time. When she was alone, she left them alone.

When she'd exited the inn today, the pip-squeak who'd been tagging along lately started making a fuss about something. She'd brought him with her (since the guy in black had gestured that she should), but of course, he was now being noisy again.

Garbage was getting sick of it, so she stopped listening.

To Raraja, this was a huge nuisance.

Damn that guy! Saying stuff like, "If you're so worried, why don't you go with her?"

Ugh...!

Raraja would never admit that he was worried about letting a girl like her go into the dungeon alone. She was the monster's leftovers after all. Even so...it was true that he'd questioned the sanity of her going underground all by herself.

And now that he'd followed her...this was how it'd turned out.

"Awoooo!!!"

"Ah, damn it! I *just* told her!"

Garbage let out a howl as she kicked in the door of a burial chamber and leaped through it.

Obviously, Raraja had no choice but to follow. He didn't want to be left alone—not in the dim light of the dungeon, where he could only see a little ways ahead—even if that meant his only companion was trash, and there would be monsters in their way.

"BOOOW?!"

"ROOAAAR!!!"

Inside the burial chamber were a number of humanoid creatures alongside burbling puddles of pink goop.

Kobolds and bubbly slimes?

If so, they were in luck. For this level of the dungeon, these were weak enemies...though still only "weak" by dungeon standards.

"Woof!!!"

But even as Raraja was thinking that, Garbage was already springing at the enemy. She was hopelessly outnumbered, but what did she care? She swung her broadsword around, slamming it into the monsters.

"AAAHHHH?!?!?!"

A scream—a spurt of blood. The thick blade struck, tearing through a dog-faced monster's shoulder and ending its life.

"Oh, for the love of…! Fine!"

Raraja ran into the action, but his joints creaked painfully.

Damn it, my body's aching! This was the fault of the cot he'd been sleeping on lately. No, more than that—it was Iarumas's fault.

When the man had learned that Raraja slept in the stables, he'd thrown him onto a cot at the inn. Raraja had tried to object, but Iarumas had simply frowned and said, "Sister Ainikki would be furious."

Okay, fair enough. That is *a scary prospect.*

Raraja could only nod in agreement because, yeah, Iarumas didn't have a lot of choice in the matter.

The wonderful thing about a cot was the fact that it was a bed, no matter how simple. Even if it was just some wooden boxes put together, a cot was leagues better than the ropes some particularly cheap inns put out to allow guests to sleep on their feet. While the straw of the stables wasn't so bad, the softness of his new sleeping arrangement surprised him.

But…

I can't get used to it…!

"Rah, ahhhh!!!"

Nonetheless, it would be a lie to say he'd gained nothing. With a shriek and a swing of his dagger, Raraja tore through the body of a kobold.

"UGHHH?!"

He kicked the dog-faced beastman away as it let out a high-pitched cry of agony. Keeping his distance, the boy sought to catch his breath.

I hit it!

There was no need for big swings—Raraja's movements were fast and sharp enough now. He just needed to focus, hone in on his enemy's weak points, then stab and pierce through them.

That was it. And in order to do it, he needed to observe his enemies more closely.

That strike just now...it was too shallow...!

"Growl!"

Meanwhile, Garbage was swinging her broadsword in all directions, unconcerned that she was covered in slime. Her strikes would only hit or crush the enemy if she got lucky. Totally aimless. Even Raraja could see that the way she fought wasn't any kind of proper technique.

And yet...the way she twisted her entire body like a spring... That move was...

Sister Ainikki's...?

It looked similar, at least.

There was a dry snapping sound, like splitting air, as a slime burst and then rained back down. One of the kobolds got caught up in her attack, and was subsequently turned to mincemeat—*oh, yikes!*

"Damn, you're scary!"

"Bark?"

"Keep on going wild like that!" As he swung around his new dagger, Raraja wondered, *Just how much of what I say does she actually understand?*

A girl with red hair, frighteningly cold blue eyes, and doglike mannerisms... The iron collar around her neck was heavy, and the broadsword she carried was like a claw—one much too big for a person of her size.

She thought nothing of killing monsters. As did Raraja. But, were they the same when it came to killing humans?

He'd heard that she had been brought to the dungeon as a slave. What was she delving for now on her own?

He couldn't imagine that she adventured out of loyalty to Iarumas. Raraja had the vague feeling that she was searching for something—or someone—down here. But as for who or what that might be...

Yeah, I've got no clue.

When Raraja finished off the last of their opponents, Garbage didn't react with any particular emotion. The nice new clothes Sister Ainikki had bought her the other day were already stained a dark red. The girl rubbed her cheek with the sleeve of her cloak, standing there as if in a daze, and then...

"Sniff… Sniff…"

"Ah, hey!"

She scrunched up her nose and ran off to one corner of the room.

Raraja chased after her, and there it was—the treasure chest.

"Yeesh… If you need something, just say so." Though it's not like Raraja's words would get through to her. He crouched down in front of the chest.

Why do these things show up anyway? That question applied to both the monsters and treasure chests.

"Because this is the dungeon" was the simple answer in both cases… but it left a lot of mysteries.

Here he was in this strange place, adventuring alongside a man in black and a redheaded girl.

Just days ago, he would've never been able to imagine living like this. It was a far cry from the time he'd spent running around as a lackey of the clan, and not just in terms of how he was treated—the people around him now were different too. Of course, it wasn't as if he understood them very well.

He wasn't going to deny that he was starting to have a little fun, though…

"Whoa?!"

Was it because he was thinking about all this stuff?

Suddenly, there was a loud clunk, and the treasure box in front of him shook violently.

A trap? His head snapped up, and there was Garbage, a cold look in her eyes.

"Yap."

She'd kicked the box as if to say, *"Get on with it."*

"Why, you!" Raraja rose shakily to his feet. "You're totally looking down on me, aren't you?!"

"Arf!"

That went without saying.

§

"Could you come along with me for a bit?"

"Sure, I don't mind."

One of the best things about Sezmar was that he'd greet you with a smile even if you talked to him while he was eating. The fighter patted the helmet he'd left by the edge of the table and looked up at the friend standing next to him.

"Thanks," Iarumas replied. The black rod—that iron scabbard—peeked out from beneath his similarly black cloak.

It was evening at Durga's Tavern.

"When can you start?" asked Iarumas.

"When do you need me by?"

"Not in any hurry, but sooner is probably better."

"Well then…"

Some nights might have been busier than others, but this tavern was always bustling, and the sound of money was in the air.

For adventurers, time was an extremely ambiguous construct. They tended to quantify it in one of three ways: when they were going to the dungeon, when they returned to town, and when they wouldn't be going to the dungeon. At any of these times, they had the option to hit up the tavern to prepare, celebrate, or rest.

That's why no one cared about Sezmar and Iarumas talking.

Iarumas the corpse-hauler was an eccentric, and so was the fighter who still called himself a knight. If these two weirdos wanted to talk, then only a real oddball would want to join that conversation.

This was especially true once the door opened and the little monster's leftovers came over to them, filthy with gore.

"Arf!" Garbage barked, perhaps announcing that she had returned.

"Yeah," Iarumas said dismissively, brushing her off. "There's food if you're hungry."

"Yap!!!"

She rushed to the round table with all the vigor of a dog wagging her tail—this caused the person who would soon be sitting with her to shout, "Hey, you! Clean yourself up first!"

"Woof?"

Yes, the complaint came from Raraja. He'd followed her into the tavern and was now griping about the blood and gore on their table. Seeing the way he scowled and muttered, Garbage looked at him cluelessly, her head tilted in a questioning manner.

Iarumas silently pushed a bowl of gruel toward the girl, and she instantly barked, "Yap!"

He then told Raraja, "Order something you like."

"Meat," the boy replied after a moment's hesitation.

Seeing how the girl dove face-first into the bowl of gruel, Sezmar cracked a bit of a smile.

"What?" asked Iarumas.

"I was thinking that you've gotten used to this." Sezmar gestured to Garbage with his chin. "Do you send her down there alone?"

"If she wants to wander off, it's really none of my concern," Iarumas replied. "And she has someone to keep an eye on her anyway."

"Guess so." Sezmar didn't press the issue.

Iarumas probably wasn't acting nonchalant to hide his embarrassment—his words expressed his genuine feelings. No doubt, he thought he was simply looking after the girl.

Sarah didn't believe it. She'd repeatedly prodded Iarumas about it while drunk, but Sezmar wouldn't do that to him. After all, Sezmar knew his strengths—he was just an honest, diligent, simple-minded, jovial guy.

"And besides, even if we ask what her goals are, it's not like we'd find out," Sezmar concluded.

"Yap?" Garbage looked up as if responding to someone calling her, but Sezmar waved his hand to say it was nothing.

Iarumas didn't even know her real name—assuming that she had one. Of course, he wouldn't know anything else either.

Having accepted this, Sezmar asked, "So, where're we headed?"

"The third floor," Iarumas responded. "I heard something about it."

"That's a shallow level."

Shallow for the dungeon, which plunged down to unknown depths; its lowest level was nestled in the deepest bowels of the earth. Even now, the third level still hadn't been fully explored. The monsters were also very different from those on the first and second floors.

"Well, for a start, I'd like to hear what you can tell me," requested Sezmar.

"From the sound of it, someone found a burial chamber behind a hidden door on the third floor."

"Oho."

"They triggered an exploding box trap that wiped out half their party. The priest hurriedly cast LOKTOFEIT to escape."

"Leaving the bodies and equipment of his party members behind, huh?" Sezmar murmured. "A *priest* survived the blast?"

"They could have been a lord instead," said Iarumas. "You get what I'm saying, though, right?"

"Yeah—there's a mound of corpses and equipment in that hidden room."

Iarumas nodded. Sezmar crossed his arms.

"You hear this from Sister Aine?"

"From a drunk who seemingly wanted people to hear."

"Well, that sounds dodgy."

"It sure does."

Iarumas and Sezmar both let out a low laugh. They hadn't forgotten what'd happened the other day. But what good would come from dwelling on it? The information on the hidden room smelled fishy and sounded dangerous...but it was still nothing compared to the usual perils of the dungeon.

And anyway, what was the difference between a sudden attack by assassins and being ambushed by monsters? They might be walking into a trap, but Sezmar was more afraid of the ones set inside treasure chests.

"Sure, count me in. Sounds fun." With his own party taking a break, this was the perfect thing to help stave off boredom. Besides, it'd be good to help out a friend.

"Thanks," Iarumas murmured. He then turned and called out to the boy thief who'd been listening. "Raraja. Are you coming too?"

The boy was in the middle of tearing into his order of meat that'd just arrived. He said nothing at first, simply wiping his mouth with his sleeve. It seemed that he was rather torn over what to do—no immediate answer came from his mouth.

Raraja's head swirled with the incident from the other day, along with the veracity of this rumor, how dodgy it seemed, and his own level of ability.

He weighed danger against profit. How risky was this?

If Sezmar was coming, they'd be safer than before. Probably.

So, after a lingering pause, he finally managed to choke out the words, "If there's money in it."

"None that's guaranteed," was the short, blunt response.

Raraja scowled, and a look of resignation bordering on desperation crossed his face. "How many people are we taking? Not six, right?"

There was an unspoken rule of the dungeon: people never adventured in groups larger than six. A variety of reasons were given for this rule, including the width of the corridors or the size of the burial chambers...but they were all things that people had come up with after the fact. The burial chambers were big enough to fit massive dragons, and sometimes the corridors felt too tight to breathe in. Therefore, in the dungeon, where space and distance were vague, the only distinction that mattered was whether you were in the front or back row.

Despite all of this speculation, there was just one true reason for the standard party size:

If a group of more than six enter, they will die.

It was a rumor, whispered as though it were fact. But everyone believed it nonetheless.

There had once been a party of ten; they'd gone down and hadn't come back up. Nor had two separate parties of six who'd met and joined forces during a dive. Same outcome.

The fates of these parties were uncertain. Some said they had been sealed inside the stone walls, while others assumed that their guts had been devoured by monsters.

This was why a party consisted of six people. No more—though fewer was fine.

And that number...included corpses.

I can see why this guy worked alone, thought Raraja. It made sense.

"Let's see... As it stands, we have three people, but..." Iarumas turned toward the girl who was scarfing down gruel in one corner of the tavern. "Will you come too?"

Garbage raised a gruel-coated face from her dish and barked in response. "Arf!"

"I see." Iarumas nodded with a pensive expression.

I don't get it...

With a disappointed look on his face, Raraja glanced at Sezmar. The knight smiled without a word then held up his fingers for Raraja to see.

Four of them.

§

The next day—first floor underground.

"Ugh, it never changes..."

You could hardly blame Raraja for scowling.

Just after they descended the stairs into the dungeon, the area was overflowing with adventurers. Here, the dungeon's impact on perception was still weak. The place was crowded, cramped, congested. Yet, if they pushed their way between the others and advanced one grid space, it would all fade away in an instant.

Garbage snarled—even she seemed somewhat exasperated.

Raraja didn't know how many adventurers here would be swallowed up by the dungeon, never to return. Nor did he care. He could become one of the lost himself.

That was something he preferred to think about as little as possible. Though, in truth, it did concern him.

"Hey," Raraja called out to the man in black walking ahead of him. "What're they all doing?"

"Treating their wounds," Iarumas answered, not bothering to turn and look at him. The man was staring straight into the darkness of the dungeon. "They rest in the stables to restore their spells, and then delve into the dungeon to use healing magic on their party."

"Okay, sure. But mages can only use spells so many times per day, right?"

"That's why they make multiple trips over several days," Iarumas explained, looking over his shoulder at Raraja for the first time. "Visit just the stables to restore magic—head to the entrance of the dungeon to heal. That's how it works."

"Seriously…?" Raraja responded with a groan. He could imagine why the other parties did it that way: lack of money.

These parties squatted on the ground, waited for their priests to cast DIOS, and then went back to the surface. It was a long process, and ultimately, one that wouldn't change even once they finished and resumed exploring.

This scene was a far cry from the heroic image that people in other regions had of adventurers.

But even so…

Things are still better than they used to be…

Raraja had started to realize the extent of how *wrong* his life had been before, but only because he had more leeway now.

However, his current party—if he could call it that, and he wasn't sure he could—didn't have anyone who could cast priest spells.

Once he'd started making money, Raraja had been able to sleep in a proper bed for the first time. Even his cot seemed like quite a luxury. In his old clan, he really hadn't gotten leeway to observe the situation around him. And, in all the time he'd adventured with them, he hadn't been healed, not once, not even a chance of it. Getting a resurrection would've been out of the question—it was cheaper to save the money and catch some new rookies instead.

There were any number of replacements for Raraja…or a girl like Garbage.

After returning from the dungeon, these placeholder adventurers would sprawl on mounds of straw, groaning on and on at the heat and pain of their wounds, only to be used as meat shields again the next day. Eventually, they would die.

He'd seen so many of his comrades go through that. And they'd been the lucky ones. After all, they'd had *some* chance of surviving.

Just as Raraja had.

Sezmar, who'd overheard their conversation about healing magic, butted into it. "What, did no one ever do it for you?" This free knight, whose armor clattered as he walked, had the heaviest equipment of anyone in the group.

"Well, uh..." Raraja trailed off. He could hardly be blamed for feeling a bit nervous. The knight was one of the most famous adventurers in this dungeon, and that put him in a league far above Raraja's. Sezmar wasn't so intimidating when he was resting at the tavern, but seeing him all suited up like this made Raraja feel the power disparity all the more keenly. The man's easygoing nature only served to make Raraja even more confused about how he should act.

I almost wish he were more unfriendly—like a certain someone—and not so easy to understand...

Raraja cast a resentful look toward Iarumas as he thought this, but the man in black had already turned and was walking away.

Since there was no point in following that train of thought, Raraja focused on Sezmar once more. "No," was his brief but honest answer.

"Then let me show you what better treatment looks like." Sezmar raised his right hand up high and chanted fluently. "Mimuarif pezanme re feiche (*O great shield, come quickly from beyond*)."

"Uh, wha...?" Raraja uttered without meaning to—but nothing happened.

"Arf...?" Even Garbage came to a stop, blinking her clear eyes repeatedly.

Though in her case, I'll bet she was probably just caught off guard because this guy suddenly started shouting...

Raraja was just as confused. Hesitantly, he looked at Sezmar, trying to get a read on the knight's reaction. "Um, what was that about?"

"If we had a good priest along, they'd chant MAPORFIC for us before we went exploring," Sezmar replied.

Up ahead, Iarumas let out a sigh. "You're not a lord, so you can't use it."

"Wah ha ha ha!" Sezmar let out a boisterous laugh.

Raraja was astonished. He didn't know *what* to say.

Uhh, so, basically...that was a joke?

It must've been. Probably. Maybe.

"Your defense (AC) isn't all about hardening yourself. Let's loosen up and take it easy!" Inside his helm, which was adorned with a dragon ornament, Sezmar winked. Or...that's what it felt like to Raraja.

Was he trying to lighten things up with a joke?

If so...then let's see if I can figure something out while the mood is relaxed.

Having made up his mind, Raraja casually asked Iarumas, "If we know where we're going, then can't we use a teleportation spell to zoom right there?"

He wasn't going off what he'd heard—Raraja wasn't all that knowledgeable about spells. Rather, he was speaking from experience; specifically, the one from the other day. That Demon's Stone had been scary, but he wished he hadn't lost it...

"That's a top-level spell," Sezmar said, sounding exasperated.

Teleportation. A secret art that allowed one to jump across dimensions. Truly, it was the sort of special technique that could only be spoken of in legends. It was different from the priest spell for rapid escape. Teleportation could take the caster wherever they wanted to go.

"Even Prospero can't use it yet... I mean, can anyone?"

"Spells are valuable," Iarumas murmured simply, then kept walking. Garbage followed.

Raraja rushed after them—though before he did, he glanced back at the entrance for a moment.

Where the adventurers had once been, he could no longer see anything. Their forms had been swallowed up by the darkness—or perhaps, it was the other way around, and Raraja and the others were the ones being swallowed.

§

"You've got skill."

"Woof?"

"It's not just monsters. You've cut down people too, right?"

"Arf!"

"I see how it is."

It was a carefree conversation…

Or it would have been, had Sezmar not just finished swinging around his Were Slayer and chopping up capybaras, giant toads, and coyotes.

With awkward movements, a gore-soaked Garbage wrapped her broadsword in her sleeve, using the fabric to wipe the blood off. The gesture was familiar to Sezmar, and he put a hand on top of the girl's head, seeming genuinely pleased.

"Woof?!"

These exchanges happened in every burial chamber they cleared—Raraja never interrupted them. He faced down the treasure chest with a serious expression on his face, focused on unsealing it.

Raraja would say that *unlocking* it was the easy part. The real problem was identifying the type of trap and knowing how to disarm it. No thief, no matter how experienced, could ever be completely sure. And… it was even worse for one who was still just getting started.

"If only we had a priest who could cast CALFO to look inside," Sezmar murmured. He glanced at Raraja, who was silently probing the box.

Sezmar then mussed Garbage's curly, red hair like he was petting a dog. She protested with a "Yap!" but he kept on doing it.

"If you were going to recruit people to come with us, shouldn't you have asked Aine along too?" Sezmar asked.

"She'd probably charge me." The answer was that simple.

The sole spellcaster of this party was standing next to the wall, his posture relaxed. So far, he'd been able to take things easier than usual—while it might've been a struggle for Garbage to fight all on her own, the enemies of the first and second underground floors were weak with Sezmar around.

There was no point in Iarumas wasting valuable spells. Along the way, he'd fallen into the back row with Raraja.

When he boasted about how nice it was to relax a bit, Sezmar laughed out loud. "I'll bet. Though you'd better not act like too much of a miser. Lives are on the line here. That's why Aine nags so much, you know?"

"I think 'sermonizes' is the better word."

"Makes sense."

Sister Ainikki, that devout elf priest, had given Iarumas a sermon a few days ago too. As Iarumas continued his idle banter with Sezmar, he vaguely recalled what'd happened in Durga's Tavern the other day.

§

"Isn't it better not to know...?"

Durga's Tavern was busy, packed with adventurers who might die today or tomorrow. At a small table, away from the noisy chatter, Aine had quietly asked this question between sips of northern distilled spirits.

"About what?" came the response.

"Your past."

Yes, the tavern was always full of adventurers—this day was no exception. After leaving Raraja and Garbage behind, Sister Ainikki had led Iarumas to a round table. Once he'd meekly taken a seat, the silver-haired elf had settled down across from him.

For drinks, Iarumas had ordered himself a simple beer. Seeing this, Aine put on a slightly troubled smile.

"I've heard about what happened the other day."

"With that 'client' of Raraja's, you mean?"

"Yes." Aine nodded, her face deathly serious. "Although it involves today's disturbance as well."

Iarumas made a habit of listening to her when she looked like this. In this world, being picky about accepting aid from others was a luxury.

"I think we can be certain that they're targeting you, or the girl," Aine continued.

"Probably."

"Then it's dangerous. For you, or for her."

"Or for both of us."

Aine paused. Hesitantly, she opened her mouth as if to speak—once, and then twice. She closed her eyes slightly, recited the name of God, and then quietly asked, "Have you ever considered it might be better not to know?"

Iarumas's response was immediate.

"I don't think so."

The noise of the tavern pressed in on them and then receded, much like the tide. For a while, neither Iarumas nor Aine said anything—it felt like each was waiting for the other to speak, but at the same time, like the conversation had come to an end.

But then, Iarumas broke that silence. "I'm grateful for your concern. Whatever I decide to do, it's going to be after I've learned about my past. Without that knowledge, I can't make a choice. Right?"

Aine didn't reply at first. She grasped what he was talking about, and smiled. Her expression was one of resignation and exasperation.

"I thought you might say that... And lately, I've started to understand."

"About what?" Iarumas asked.

"Your way."

"My way?"

"Yes." Aine clasped her hands in her lap, shifting around in her seat. Then, she raised her pretty index fingers. "You know good. You know evil. You're not pure, and yet, at the same time, are not wholly corrupted." Her face—still beautiful, even though she would not live as long as her kind once did—looked straight at Iarumas. "That's why you can choose neutrality."

"Maybe I'm just stumbling along the middle of the road."

"Perhaps."

Aine sighed and her eyes narrowed gently. Seeing this, Iarumas shrugged.

"Come to think of it, you've never suggested that I should abandon Garbage."

"Of course not," Aine replied, pursing her lips indignantly. The gesture instantly erased the elven maturity of her face, leaving behind only a girl who looked her age. It was funny how that worked.

She stared off into the distance at Raraja and Garbage, who were surrounded by more experienced adventurers.

"You just try and do it," she challenged. "If you start tilting toward evil, I'll pull you back to this side."

"That, or just shove me over the edge and then finish me."

"Aren't you grateful?"

"You're making me tear up here."

147

Iarumas laughed, and Sister Ainikki smiled, albeit somewhat awkwardly.

Iarumas felt himself wanting to talk—not because of Aine's earnestness, but for no particular reason. He hadn't been hiding things. Nor had he meant to keep quiet.

It's just that now, he thought, *I can tell her.*

Perhaps this was because of the devout saint's virtue.

"Sister Ainikki."

"Yes?" Her silver hair swayed as she tilted her head to the side. "What is it?"

"You're mistaken about two things…"

§

With a clunk, the lid of the treasure chest fell to the ground, snapping Iarumas back to the present.

Raraja wiped the sweat from his forehead and let out a long breath. "It's a success, then?"

"Well, sure. Poison needles are easy…" Raraja boasted, but it was clear to see that he was exhausted.

The thief's work unlocking chests was always tense—very much like the combat that always came beforehand. If the thief failed to disarm the trap, *they* were the person who'd get hurt. And in some cases, traps could be instantly lethal. If a trap was misidentified, then all the thief's work was just paving the road toward their ultimate demise.

Even when there was a priest around, as was mentioned earlier, disarming was still a one-man battle, and no one could be relied upon for help.

"Yap!"

That's why Raraja felt exhausted. Garbage just ignored him to pounce on the treasure.

Not that she understood the value of it—no.

"Arf! Arf!"

It sparkled and was pretty, so maybe she understood its worth in the most pure and innocent way possible.

She stuck her hands into the mound of gold coins in the chest and stirred them up. Satisfied, the girl headed over to Iarumas.

"Ruff!" She barked proudly, holding up a single gold coin as if to say, *"How's that?"*

"For you, this is just another trophy, huh?"

"Woof?!"

When Iarumas patted her on the head with his gauntleted hand, she let out a cry of protest. This kind of exchange, where she looked up at him and growled resentfully as he held her head down, was typical for them.

It was the same for Raraja, who sat on the floor, gulping from his waterskin without concern for how much was left.

"No drinking until we're through the next burial chamber," Sezmar said with a laugh. Raraja let out an exaggerated groan.

"It sure is a hike to the third floor…"

"We *could* use the elevator…but then we'd miss out on all the treasure along the way…"

When Sezmar put it that way, Raraja, who was still a newcomer to the dungeon, couldn't argue with him. After all, the knight was one of the adventurers who'd made it the farthest in the dungeon. And Iarumas probably had a wealth of experience too.

As for Garbage…

"Arf?"

"It's nothing…"

The girl looked at him, head tilted questioningly. She seemed to be thinking, *"I'm not so sure about that."*

Well, when it came down to it, Raraja wouldn't have wanted to miss out on the treasure either. In his old clan, he wouldn't have seen a coin of it, but in this party, he could count on it being divvied up properly.

The warm feeling that came from having a full coin purse was not so easy to relinquish once you got used to it.

As if he saw through Raraja, Sezmar clapped the boy on the shoulder. "Still, for all your complaints, you're pretty used to this, aren't you?"

"Well, it's not as tough as taking on a dragon…" That battle had been intense. He never wanted to go through one like it again. But, being an adventurer, he inevitably would.

Raraja let out a deep sigh, provoking a muffled laugh from inside Sezmar's helmet. It was clear the knight was teasing him, but not in a mocking way. There was something strangely jovial about it.

That's why Raraja's resentful gaze was focused not on him, but next to Garbage (who, for her part, was just standing around vacantly), on the man in black. Iarumas was stuffing the treasure into a sack.

"I've been wondering for a while now…" said Raraja.

"What?"

"Which is it?" Raraja asked in an exhausted tone, his elbow resting on his knee and his cheek in his palm. "Are you a mage who can fight, or a fighter who can cast spells?"

"Who can say?"

That inscrutable answer provoked an awfully fascinating look on Raraja's face. Garbage leaned in to look at his expression with a confused, "Arf?"

And just like that, their exploration continued on smoothly.

§

"This the place?" Sezmar asked.

Iarumas nodded. "Seems like it."

In front of the party stood a stone wall, though there was nothing particularly noteworthy about it. However, its appearance was hard to pin down—it looked like a single smooth sheet of rock, a wall of piled stones, and a rock wall, seemingly all at once.

Down here in the dungeon, an adventurer's perception was a vague and uncertain thing. The one understanding they all shared was that this wall was made of stone, and it was in a corridor connecting two burial chambers.

Raraja hesitantly approached the wall with Garbage—who was sniffing the air—beside him.

"Okay… I'm gonna check it, all right?"

"Please do," said Iarumas.

Raraja touched the wall, searching it for anything that felt out of place.

It was well known that there were secret doors in the dungeon. There were also one-way doors and doors that couldn't normally be unlocked. Although he didn't understand how they worked...

Raraja remained silent as he looked over the stone, feeling quite tense. Fortunately for him, it was unheard of for doors themselves to be booby-trapped. Though if there were monsters, they'd be on the other side...

Swallowing his spit, Raraja felt the wall for a while, patting it, until he heard Garbage yawning next to him. Then, drawing his dagger, he ran it along one corner of the wall, cutting out the shape of a door.

"That should do it... I think."

"Nicely done," Sezmar said, giving him genuine praise. Raraja rubbed his nose bashfully, not saying anything in return.

The front-liners would have to take it from here. The boy backed away slowly, letting the fighters move up.

Sezmar, Garbage, and then Iarumas.

Iarumas seemed relaxed as he looked at the hidden door, his hand on the hilt of his katana that looked like a black rod.

"Better mark this on the map," he said, the corners of his lips turning up. It wasn't clear what was so funny. "Do we go in?"

"You're the leader," Sezmar said casually. "Go ahead."

"Okay."

"Woof!"

Having received permission, Garbage slammed herself into the door, and the adventurers rushed into the burial chamber.

Most burial chambers contained monsters called guardians...as well as treasure. The party needed to remain alert because, even if the monsters had already been killed, they would reappear after some time. They searched the inside of the dark burial chamber, each of them honing all five of their senses.

Smells, sounds, flickering shadows. The taste of iron on the tips of their tongues. The flow of air against their skin.

It was a tense moment...but nothing happened.

"They're…not here?" Raraja let out an unintentional sigh as he relaxed.

"Maybe," Iarumas said briefly. "Let's look for bodies."

"And their treasure and equipment?"

"You get what it's all about."

That was a compliment. Or so Raraja thought for a second. Though, he wasn't sure *why* he'd thought that. Regardless, the boy did as he was told and looked around the burial chamber for the dead bodies of adventurers.

Garbage, however, did not.

"Arf…!"

She'd been on edge with the anticipation of battle and was now blatantly disappointed by the lack of it. However, though she kicked at the stone-tiled floor out of boredom, there was someone who hadn't let go of his weapon.

"There're no monsters," Sezmar murmured, sword in hand. "No corpses I can see either."

"I expected as much." Iarumas was the same. He chuckled, hand still on the black rod that held his weapon of choice.

"This is getting interesting."

"You said it."

Raraja came back, grumbling, after a short run around the room. "There's nothing here, okay? Don't you think it was a fake tip?"

That's when it happened.

It was sudden. Ear-piercing, high-pitched. A metallic noise echoed through the burial chamber.

Garbage let out a surprised squawk, but she could hardly be blamed for that. As the girl clasped her hands to her ears, Raraja reflexively drew his dagger and got ready for a fight.

"Wh-Wha…?!"

"An alarm, huh?" Sezmar muttered. "Even though we didn't open a chest?"

"It's not as though there are no rooms like that," Iarumas said. "I wonder if an examiner's going to show up."

"What's that…?!" Raraja shouted. But then…

A shadow moved.

The endless darkness that filled the dungeon swelled up, took tangible form, and lunged.

In that instant, the monsters attacked!

§

"Uh, oh, oh, wha, ah?!"

A silver flash tore through the darkness and Raraja reflexively swung his dagger to deflect it.

The impact knocked him onto his backside, and the blade rapidly followed after him. He screamed and jumped out of the way, but there was no doubt that the attack had ground down his focus (HP).

"Wh-What *are* these guys?!"

The monsters that had appeared out of the darkness were human in shape.

Could they be adventurers? They were humans, wearing mixed equipment, and they had a bizarre light shining in their eyes. There seemed to be no end to them—group after group poured out of the gloom of the burial chamber.

"Let's run, okay?!" Raraja screamed. "We're gonna die!!!"

"There's no escape while the alarm's ringing."

The creatures slowly closed in, swinging at them mercilessly.

Iarumas parried a slash with his blade, turning it aside, and then there was a flash as he mowed through the enemy's torso.

The clear sound of steel on steel. The splash of blood.

One of them went down.

"This takes me back," Iarumas remarked, flicking the blood from his katana and adjusting his stance. However, those words seemed to catch even him by surprise.

It...*takes me back?* Iarumas repeated in his mind.

"You know them?" asked Sezmar, who was slashing at any enemy adventurers who came too close.

Iarumas could only shake his head at Sezmar's question. "It just feels that way. And I think that time...I was a little deeper than this."

"What's that supposed to mean?" Sezmar was smiling. This free knight—this fighter—always was. He blocked the enemy's attacks with his big shield, and then his Were Slayer roared. There were only humans here, but humans were animals too, and they were all equal before the sharpness of its blade.

He swung once, then twice in quick succession, carving up a fighter that had carelessly gotten within striking range. But Sezmar, of course, understood how to maintain his advantage.

"I want to finish this before they get any spells off," he declared. "Hey, Iarumas. Got any good magic you can use?"

"Wish I could silence them...like a priest with MONTINO," Iarumas replied casually, but his empty left hand hadn't begun forming signs yet.

If he was going to use a spell, it would be LAHALITO, or...

Perhaps an even higher-level spell, like BACORTU, or MADALTO.

However, BACORTU's fizzle field only lowered the force of incoming magic. If he was going to cast something that high-level, then freezing them with MADALTO was the better bet. There were no casters among the enemies, at least within visual range. But that didn't mean there weren't any in the back, still yet to be identified.

Besides, he couldn't count on BACORTU to affect the reinforcements that the alarm kept bringing in. The same would obviously apply if he mowed down all of the enemies in the chamber with a blizzard, so it didn't tilt the scales one way or the other.

No, the reason Iarumas hesitated didn't have anything to do with conserving spells. If he became defenseless in front of his enemies, that would grind down his nerves (HP) a fair bit.

I don't want to throw any moves away, he thought. *I want to make the optimal move.*

As long as there were no spells or breath weapons, the party wasn't going to collapse outright, even if the enemy acted before Iarumas.

Their party, led by two experienced adventurers, was instantly back in fighting formation. Although...Garbage was just going wild, and all Raraja could do at the moment was parry.

The only ones who could truly look at the situation and give orders were Sezmar and Iarumas. The party might be in danger, but just as long as neither of them got their heads lopped off, they weren't at a disadvantage.

Sure, one or two in the group might die, but...

"Death is no reason to stop being an adventurer," Iarumas said boldly. And he was right...just as long as there was someone left to bring the bodies back to the temple and pay the tithe.

But, even though his statement was true, it was no reason to actively choose death. A permanent end would come on its own, in due time.

I see. The things Aine says do have some meaning.

If he were to die because of a careless move in battle, that priest would be absolutely livid with him.

As Iarumas rushed around the battlefield, his head full of thoughts, he looked toward the girl.

"Woof!!!"

Garbage was in her element. Like a fish in water, or perhaps, a hound chasing prey. She jumped into the enemy formation with a loud bark, taking advantage of the weight of her sword to mow them down. It looked like the blade was swinging her petite frame around, but the reverse was actually true.

It was difficult to believe that someone as slender as Garbage could support such a hefty blade, but she was slamming it into her enemies with all its weight and momentum.

Reaping bodies, crushing heads, sending limbs flying—that wasn't any proper kind of swordsmanship.

Without hesitation, Iarumas called out to the violent storm of blood.

"Garbage!"

"Arf!"

He didn't call out to say anything meaningful. He figured that, even if he told her to come back or to stand down, she wouldn't understand him.

But if he called her name...she'd respond. She'd stop, turn, and raise her head.

Those clear blue eyes looked straight at him. Iarumas even thought he could see his own reflection in them.

Then, suddenly, they sank.

"Yap?!"

"Wha…?!"

Garbage screamed. Even Iarumas cried out in surprise.

A chute.

The floor opened under Garbage's feet, swallowing her up.

Strange.

Time seemed to stretch on. A single drop of blood flew toward Iarumas. He could follow its arc with his eyes.

It wasn't the first time Garbage had stepped on that spot of floor.

She had been jumping, running around, and swinging her sword this entire time. If the chute was triggered by weight, it would have gone off at the first step.

So why? Why did it open now? Because she stopped? Was it targeting her? If so, that meant…

Someone's controlling the dungeon?

"Hah!" Iarumas smiled. It was a hungry smile, like that of a shark that had found its prey.

In the next instant, he kicked off the floor of the burial chamber, jumping into the air. Slipping between the shadowlike monsters, he threw the katana that was hanging in his right hand.

Its blade caught the gap in the floor just as the chute was closing, and the metal began emitting an unpleasant creaking sound.

"Iarumas?!"

The strange noise of his groaning katana—Sezmar's shout.

None of it mattered to Iarumas.

He seized the grip of his katana with both hands and started using it to force the floor open.

"Hey," Iarumas said. "Once you've cut your way out of here, take the stairs down."

"What are you going to do?" Now that Iarumas and Garbage were out of formation, Sezmar was moving to fill the holes that they'd left in the front row. He bashed an enemy with his large shield and stood next to Raraja.

"I'm jumping in," Iarumas stated simply. He laughed, then continued, "You can go home if you like…"

"You'd be fine with that?"

"I can't ask you to follow me to your death."

As Iarumas twisted one foot into the gap, he looked at Sezmar.

As Sezmar twisted the Were Slayer into his opponent's ribs, impaling them through the heart, he looked at Iarumas.

They both let out empty laughs and shared goofy smiles.

Seeing the two of them act like this, Raraja, who was swinging his dagger for dear life, looked incredulous.

But that, too, only lasted a moment.

Raraja worked up all the courage he could, and then, with a pensive look on his face, he asked, "You're going down there to save that girl?"

"No…not really…?" Iarumas glanced at Raraja, then pushed down hard with his foot, opening enough space for one person to enter the gap.

Raraja could tell immediately that Iarumas wasn't just joking around or attempting to deny his motivations.

The man genuinely had no intention—none—of saving her.

Then why?!

It made no sense. Despite his confusion, Raraja still shouted, "This is crazy, okay?! You're making no sense!"

Yeah. It made no sense. Why do it? What was going on here?

Suddenly, a semblance of understanding formed in his mind…

"You're up against the master of the dungeon, right?!" cried Raraja.

Iarumas's answer was short.

"I have business with them."

And so, with well-practiced moves, as if he'd done it dozens of times…

Iarumas jumped down the chute and vanished.

§

"Awooooo!!!"

Her cry echoed hollowly in the darkness before fading away.

Garbage sat on the cold stone tiles of the dark dungeon floor, peering around at her surroundings.

No one was there.

"Woof..." The girl gave an indifferent little snort. She was used to cold, dark, stone rooms. As for being on her own...well, she always had been. This was nothing new.

For some time, Garbage sat around in a daze. Then, she stood up straight and quietly walked off.

No—she didn't understand what had happened or anything complicated like that. Nor did she have any idea what she should do about it. Her mind never lingered on what was to come, or what had come before, but rather, on what was happening right now.

And yet, because of this situation...

For the first time in a long while, Garbage was remembering the past.

One day, all of a sudden, she'd been pulled out of a dark room and stuffed into a box that shook back and forth. The container had shuddered with an extra-large jolt, and then...Garbage had been cast out into a wide-open space.

Strange things had attacked. She hadn't understood them, but she'd killed to avoid being killed herself. Someone had offered her food. They'd put a collar on her. She'd decided to obey for as long as the food kept coming. They'd said *go*—she'd delved into the dungeon. They'd said *kill*—she'd killed.

The stone ceiling down here suited her much better than the strangely wide blue one up there (not that she'd even seen that one until they pulled her from the dark room).

Yeah. Before, she hadn't thought her situation was so bad.

But she'd been hungry. Truly, absolutely, famished.

Meeting these new people had surprised her. For the first time, she'd been able to eat as much as she liked. Nobody had gotten mad. It'd been a new experience. And it wasn't just the food—before, Garbage couldn't remember many instances when she hadn't been ordered around.

Because of this new leeway, Garbage had been thinking that she might stick around a bit longer. But, if she was going to be separated from them, then she figured, well, there probably wasn't much she could do about it.

Being with them wasn't so bad, she thought, although not in such well-formed words.

After some time silently and aimlessly wandering the dungeon, the girl suddenly came to a stop. She was in a vast space. However, it didn't appear to be what adventurers called a burial chamber—no doors were blocking it off.

A corridor. A space. There were any number of things it could have been called…

Garbage spat distastefully. Her nose was picking up an unpleasant stench in the back of the area.

"If you'd just died, this would have been much easier. But you *had* to keep on clinging to your filthy life…"

Thoroughly unamused. The source of the smell emerged from the depths of the darkness. It was a man wearing a *high-quality robe.*

He wasn't alone.

Men in black garb followed him, emerging from the shadows.

Countless men.

Countless.

They pushed toward Garbage as one mass, encircling her in a crowd several layers deep.

Garbage held the hilt of her broadsword tight, slowly lowering her posture.

The men seemed unthreatened. They closed in. The horrid smell was getting awfully strong.

"To think I'd need to bring out this amulet just to dispose of a feral mutt like you…"

The robed man at the front of the group spat his words out hatefully. There was a strange thing hanging around his neck, some sort of shard—an amulet, bearing a searing white light within.

"You've gotten out of hand. We can't have you making a name for yourself."

The man clutched the amulet, letting out a groan as he fixed his eyes on Garbage. There was no hostility in them. No remorse either. Just contempt and pique at the fact that this bothersome task had come his way.

As the man spoke, Garbage heard the others around him loosening swords in the scabbards beneath their robes.

"You're just a little mutt of a girl. There is no point in speaking to an animal that cannot understand, but…die here."

The man was right about one thing—Garbage didn't understand a word he said. She wasn't listening.

No, she just absolutely loathed the stench that clung to these men. When she'd been in that small, dark, cold room, it was the one smell that had always bothered her. They would appear occasionally, look at her, say something, and then leave. At some point, Garbage had come to recognize them by their stink.

That's why, ever since she'd been thrown out of the box into that wide-open place…she had been doing just one thing for herself.

Whenever someone cloaked in that stench appeared, Garbage always thought—

"Die, accursed bastard of the *Llylgamyn Royal House!*"

—*I'll get rid of them.*

§

With each grunting swing of her broadsword, another corpse was added to the pile.

"Growl…!"

Garbage's will to fight showed no sign of flagging. The silent assassins came at her, slicing with drawn blades, but she didn't retreat a single step. She sprang toward the middle of the group encircling her, swinging her broadsword without precision—if she got lucky, someone would get cut open by her wild slashes.

The wind roared as she stepped in with her blade—she used one thin leg to support herself as she hurtled her massive sword all the way around. This was no proper swordcraft, not by any means. It was forceful and violent, relying on weight and mass.

Nonetheless, she danced.

With every unchoreographed step, every whirl of her sword, more bodies piled up. It was the dance of death.

This was in contrast to the assassins, who attacked in silence.

"Grrrrr!" Garbage growled as she saw that the men in robes—daggers poised and ready to strike—remained unshaken, no matter how many of their number she killed.

The assassins moved deftly, their blades always seeking her vitals. Although it was a struggle, she'd so far been able to dodge. Adventuring meant always being accompanied by death. However, when death pursued her so relentlessly, the strain was huge.

Her will was ground down. Her focus scattered. She became winded. Sweat ran down her body. Shallow, panting breaths.

"Woof!!!"

Despite her fatigue, Garbage bared her fangs, rousing herself to action, and lunged at her next prey.

No matter how many adversaries there were, their numbers couldn't be infinite. Garbage didn't understand difficult concepts like infinity, but she did grasp one thing: if she killed enough, they'd all be dead.

And yet…though the girl was an excellent fighter, she was no more than that.

"You really are a beast," snapped the robed man, not bothering to hide his contempt. "I see you have no ability to do more than thrash around wildly."

It would still take some time for her blade to reach him through the wall of onrushing assassins.

"Rrruff!!!" Garbage barked as if to say, *"Just you wait!"*

The robed man didn't bother to engage with her. Instead, he clasped the amulet hanging from his neck and began chanting words of true power.

"Seenzanme chuzanme re darui (*Unseen demons, take form*)."

Instantly, something changed.

Carried by the wind, there came an awful smell…like rotting flesh. It filled the room in no time, tainting Garbage's lungs.

"Yap?!"

For the first time, the girl's face twisted in dismay. But the true terror was yet to come.

"GRAAAHHHHGG..."

"RRAAAAUUUUGGHH!!!"

The flesh of the dead assassins began rotting and sloughing off. Yet despite this, they slowly began to rise once more...as if alive.

These rotting corpses were clearly hostile. The spell the man had chanted was SOCORDI, though Garbage didn't know this. And even if she had known, she would still, doubtlessly, have been left gaping at its incredible power.

This was indeed fifth level magic—one of the legendary mage spells which invited several monsters into this world from another.

Yes, that's right. Only *several*. SOCORDI did not have the nigh inhuman power to raise every one of the dozens of fallen corpses.

"Grr...!"

Even as they converged on her, the girl kept hold of her broadsword and never let up her resistance. She never even paused to breathe. Instinctively, she perhaps knew that stopping would mean her death.

It was a praiseworthy display. Nothing to be taken lightly.

Mired in sweat and dark red blood, she still thrust on toward her target, as if she herself were a blade.

However, even that pure and noble beauty was meaningless in this place.

"Kafaref tai nuunzanme (*Stop, O soul, thy name is sleep*)."

"Eek?!"

The spell KATINO was merciless. With a yelp, Garbage suddenly tripped over her feet and fell pitifully to the stone-tiled floor. Convulsing and thrashing around like a drowning man, she struggled to rise to her feet, but it was all futile. Her whole body had relaxed, refusing to move as she willed it.

At that very moment, her will was slipping away.

The dead surrounded her, reaching out with their hands. Her blue eyes opened wide; her mouth bobbed open and shut.

"It's kill or be killed..." the robed man murmured, greatly satisfied by the effect of his first level spell.

The mage's name? Egam Evif.

For Egam, this mission was nothing. He'd wanted no part of it. He had studied magic. Mastered the path. He'd sought glory in the palace, only to be forced to deal with this beastly girl.

However, even the highest levels of magic a mage might attain in the outside world were the most basic of basics here in the dungeon.

That fact, aggravated by how long he'd spent acquiring this spell, vexed him horribly. Regardless, the great effect it had, even here in the dungeon, filled him with pride. He was upset that so many of his secret agents had been slain by one little girl, but...

In the end, she will grovel before me, beg for forgiveness, then die like the dog she is.

"Who could have imagined? The girl His Highness left with child after that risky dalliance... She carried the blood of the accursed overlord in her veins."

The little waif swinging her sword was truly horrible, beastly. The existence of the legendary accursed mad overlord was a shame...one that had to be covered up.

Soon, the overlord's blood would be torn apart. Devoured. Banished from this world. And only the legitimate blood of the royal family would remain.

This was unquestionably a great accomplishment.

Egam narrowed his eyes, not wanting to miss the moment of triumph, and then—

"Mimuarif mimuzanmere raiseen (*Ride my voice, O terror, and spread*)!"

—his eyes snapped wide open as those true words were spoken.

"ARAAAAGUU?!?!?!"

"AAAAAAHHHHH?!"

"Wha...?!"

Egam was not the only one shocked—the effect swiftly spread through the ranks of the dead. The corpses had never been organized in the first place, but instinct had been driving them to swarm the girl. Now they all reared back or doubled over, thrashing around as they screamed.

"That spell… MAMORLIS?!"

Egam knew what it was. A mage spell of the fifth level. It shook up the spirit, inspiring terror. It even affected the dead, who had only the smallest lingering dregs of a soul.

But…

He's good, Egam thought with a groan. Oh, yes. The spell would have no effect on the nearly unconscious girl.

The caster who had shut down his rotting corpses with a single move emerged from the darkness of the dungeon.

The man in black.

In his hand, the black rod flashed, sending heads flying.

The adventurer continued straight onward, kicking away the corpses as they crumbled to ashes, then treading over them. What had first looked like a staff was, in fact, a saber. It howled.

"Mimuarif kafaref nuuni tazanme (*Struck by storms, shatter like a rock*)!"

His drawn blade harbored lethal magic, and its invisible strike scythed through the air. Egam was defenseless as his body absorbed the death spell, MAKANITO.

Slash. It was that easy.

The robed man was sent flying, his torso cleft in twain with a diagonal cut.

"Arf?" Garbage let out a small, ragged bark as she sensed the man standing right next to her. Shaking her head, she rose totteringly to her feet. Her clothes were torn. Her equipment, damaged. But she still had her broadsword in hand.

Her will to fight was unwavering. Now, as for why that was…

"I've heard it told…that in the far east, there are fighters who can also use magic…" Egam murmured, despite clearly having been bisected.

His amulet shone with a pale light, which instantly reconnected the severed halves of his body, stitching them together. The blood he'd shed, the organs he'd lost—they were all sucked back into him, returned to where they belonged.

It was an unnatural sight.

Soon, Egam stood up, unfazed, looking just as he had from the beginning. Then, peering at the adventurer beside the girl—Egam's eyes narrowed.

"Samurai, was it? I didn't know your kind still existed."

"I don't know about you either. Except for one thing." Iarumas, the black-clad samurai, smiled as if he'd just met up with an old friend. "That's an amulet, isn't it?"

"In that case…it would seem I cannot leave you alive." Without realizing it, Egam tightly grasped the shard—the amulet—that was hanging from his neck. There was a pale, dim light leaking from it. The sparkle of magic. The light of intelligence. Power made manifest.

This treasure, given to him when he received this mission, filled Egam with delight.

There was no way that he, its bearer, would end his life here. No, certainly not in this miserable dungeon, never having amounted to more than an errand boy for the royal family.

He would grow stronger. Rise to greater heights.

Seeing Egam's face drunk on his own ambition, Iarumas let out a small snort. He then turned to Garbage. "Are you good to go?" he asked the girl, whose breathing was still ragged. She kept sticking her tongue out, only to take shallow breaths.

Garbage looked up at Iarumas as if in a daze. Her clear blue eyes began to focus.

The girl was silent for a few moments out of hesitation, or because she was thinking, or perhaps for some other reason entirely. Finally, she answered him with a succinct, "Arf!"

"Good."

Iarumas's gauntleted hand patted Garbage lightly on the head. The girl did not raise her voice in protest. Instead, she gripped her broadsword tight, looking at Egam.

"Woof!!!"

§

"What *is* he?" Raraja murmured. The words slipped out unbidden as he continued exploring alone with Sezmar.

"Exploring" was putting it nicely. In truth, they were just fighting off enemies that kept coming at them. These groups consisted of fighters, mages, priests, and thieves—their black clothes were reminiscent of Hawkwind's.

Raraja was desperate. He swung his dagger, blocked, deflected, and dodged. Instantly, Sezmar's sword, the Were Slayer, howled and dealt death to their enemies.

If any spells came at the pair, they were dead. And knowing that, Raraja couldn't slack off. If he hadn't tried melding into the shadows, getting behind their attackers, and ramming his dagger through their vitals, the two of them would've probably died much sooner.

Is it different, here in the dungeon?

Strangely, he didn't hesitate to kill them. This was nothing like the time they'd been attacked in the item shop. Was it because he was thinking that these weren't men, but monsters?

Raraja crept up behind a mage whose eyes were as lightless as his own had once been and planted a dagger in his back. As the man crumpled and Raraja jumped away, it suddenly occurred to him that he had more leeway than before...

The leeway to open his mouth and speak.

"Well, what do *you* think he is?" Sezmar asked, almost as if they were just shooting the breeze. His Were Slayer cut down another foe. In the time it had taken for a desperate Raraja to dispatch one enemy, Sezmar had piled up a mountain of corpses.

The nonchalant way they were talking as they fought made Raraja mentally overlap himself with Iarumas. Attempting to banish that image from his mind, the boy said, "I've heard he's got amnesia."

Raraja and Iarumas were too different. No...the gulf in their skills was too wide.

"I've also heard a rumor that he was resurrected by mistake."

"Well, that one's not wrong," Sezmar replied, suddenly stopping at the end of a swing. He seemed to have let out a slight chuckle. "I'm also pretty curious about who he is. But I already know *what* he is."

"What...?"

"He's a *corpse*." Sezmar laughed. "A corpse we found inside an unexplored region of the dungeon."

"That's…" Raraja stopped, struggling to speak. Impossible? Unbelievable? Those words nearly tumbled from his lips. After all, if Iarumas was found as a corpse in an unexplored area…then that meant he'd been somewhere no one had reached…

"Yeah. And the scary thing is, he's definitely an *adventurer*." In a gesture that was so typical of him, Sezmar shouldered his sword, laughing. Then, turning it over in the palm of his hand, he blindly impaled an enemy that had been closing in on his flank. Sezmar didn't even turn around. The black-clad shadow he'd run through—an assassin who'd been aiming for his neck—died without even a scream.

Raraja shook his head at what he'd just seen. Then, opening his eyes wide, he refocused on the battle.

There was a mage over there. Raraja held his breath, erased his presence, and slowly crept up behind the spellcaster. The man let out a mute scream, muffled by Raraja's hand, as his throat was slit. The boy thief kept his ears perked up all the while.

"So, anyway, we brought the corpse back and tried to resurrect it… and that's how it happened!"

Sezmar carved a path for the two of them, and it was like they were walking through an empty field. Their opponents weren't beasts, but apparently that didn't matter in the face of Sezmar's blade. Or perhaps, as far as his beast-slaying sword was concerned, men were also beasts. It was still sharp after drinking their blood.

The sword swung left and right, cutting down foes as Sezmar made steady progress toward the exit to the burial chamber.

Any spellcasters?

It looked like he'd gotten all of them. Raraja quickly followed behind Sezmar, focused on defending the knight's back. Though, he doubted that he needed to.

A blade swung down toward Raraja, and he parried with his dagger. Sparks flew. His hand felt numb. But that was all.

His focus (HP) wasn't about to run out. That kind of made him happy.

"Then is it true? He's got no memories?!"

"He seems to remember how to fight, but his memories (levels) are all gone. That's no lie. But…"

"Hm?"

"I see it's been bothering you…not being able to figure out his background. And of course it would." Sezmar bisected a fighter standing between them and the door with a single slash. He laughed.

"Because he hasn't got a background."

§

"Seenzanme chuzanme re darui (*Unseen demons, take form*)."

The battle began with Egam's second SOCORDI. What difference could the addition of one more adventurer make? None, not when faced against the limitless magical power within the amulet.

"GRAAAHHHHGG…"

"RRAAAAUUUUGGHH!!!"

The dead rose again. Not just the dead—among them were also assassins, called out from the depths of darkness.

All of them were now dominated by the power of the pale light that shone from the amulet. These puppets to Egam's will attacked the adventurers, the same as they had before.

The assassins aimed for vital points with practiced daggerwork, while the dead instinctively tried to bite and tear them to pieces.

"Avoid them."

"Woof!"

Iarumas and Garbage, on the other hand, had completely changed their strategy.

The way Iarumas formed signs with his left hand made it look like he had done it tens, maybe hundreds of times before. He followed Garbage as she raced past him, and then he began chanting the true words of the spell.

"La'arif hea lai tazanme (O flames, become a storm and blow violently)!"

Searing wind raised by LAHALITO dyed the dungeon in its colors.

The recently arisen dead didn't stand a chance against the intense flames of this fourth level spell. They were wreathed in fire before they even had time to scream, and their bodies burned like torches until they turned to ash and crumbled.

"Foo! Oh!!!" Garbage shouldered her broadsword and leaped onto the trail that had been blazed by the spell. Using her momentum, she slammed the big sword down in front of her as if she were throwing it. Then, without so much as a glance at the assassin she had just cleft in twain, she used the recoil to spin around.

Taking another step forward, she swung her blade horizontally at the next enemy's torso. His spine audibly snapped. Blood and guts spilled out, staining the girl with more gore, but all that did was rile up her will to fight even more.

If she slowed, it would dull her blade. Garbage jumped in, fangs bared, like a wild animal.

"It would be a pain if the dead paralyzed us..."

Iarumas's drawn sword howled as the assassins he'd cut down rose again as undead. The one-handed swings of his katana severed heads, reducing them all to ash, extinguishing their souls. Iarumas should have been using his spells to deal with the mage quickly. The assassins were no problem as long as he kept them from striking his vitals. Truly, they were no match for a storied adventurer like Iarumas, or someone naturally gifted like Garbage.

No match, except for the fact that...

I have the amulet in my hands, thought Egam.

The mage's face was brimming with confidence. As long as he held the amulet, he could never lose.

He saw it now. A samurai, yes. The man's strength was impressive, but he wouldn't be able to unleash many more powerful spells. Of course, his sword arm was to be feared too, but still, it wasn't a problem if Egam didn't let him get close.

Keep some distance—let the monsters wear them down. Nothing had changed about Egam's plan. He had the amulet, after all. Infinite power. Limitless swarms of monsters at his disposal.

He could keep this up forever.

No matter how many they killed, all he had to do was summon more to attack them again. No matter how long it took, in the end, he would emerge victorious.

Really?

Egam was silent. At that moment, something whispered inside his brain—a sixth sense, or perhaps some instinct he'd received from the amulet.

Is that really how it is?

He could see Iarumas and Garbage still fighting hard. Blades roared. Spells flew. The dead turned to ash, and assassins died, only for their corpses to rise again.

The situation hadn't changed. Though the pair of adventurers were slowly closing in on him, that was all they were doing.

But...

With mute shock, Egam noticed Iarumas's eyes on him. The samurai's dark pupils seemed ready to swallow him.

There's something going on here...

That look—not of resignation, or of desperation, but of some other inscrutable feeling—shot through Egam.

"Daruila tazanme (*O darkness, come*)!"

Clasping the amulet tightly, Egam loudly chanted the true words of an incantation.

DILTO. The secret art which shrouds an area in darkness...was only a basic, second level spell in the dungeon. However, at the same time, the amulet spread and amplified the true words' effect to a terrifying degree.

It birthed true darkness—a dark zone, bereft of any light.

Hidden away inside it, Egam's form vanished from all perception. His very presence became undetectable.

"Woof!"

Did the girl mean to run? Or was she declaring that she wouldn't let him escape? Garbage barked, urgency apparent in her voice. She seemed ready to jump into the darkness, but...

"Wait." Iarumas's gauntleted hand caught her by the shoulder, and he pulled her back.

"Yelp?!" Garbage's eyes wavered between emotions as she barked and glared up at him resentfully.

Confusion? Objection? Or perhaps, doubt?

Instead of responding, Iarumas said in a low voice, "Figure out where he is before you go kill him."

Then, a moment later, the man in black leaped, joining the darkness.

Instantly, all five of his senses vanished. The ground, the walls, the enemy, himself—all of it melted away and dissolved.

Even a well-trained samurai was powerless inside a zone like this.

Enemies pressed in on all sides—Iarumas couldn't even tell if they were assassins or the dead.

In the next moment, Iarumas was cut all over.

Stabbed and bitten. Organs gouged. Blood flowing freely.

These were fatal wounds, no doubt. The only reason he didn't collapse was that the enemies' weapons that had impaled him were holding him upright.

But...

"Whether I can see you or not doesn't matter," Iarumas stated.

He was smiling. Suddenly, Sister Ainikki's face flashed through his mind, and his own voice played back in his ears.

You're mistaken about two things...

The other day, Iarumas had told her. Why did he venture into the dungeon? What was his reason?

Aine had sat up straight, staring at him.

Your first misunderstanding—though I do want to regain my past (levels), that is only a means to an end. The second? I am certainly searching for my former comrades, but they're also a means to an end.

The man in black's words echoed across the room.

"Iarumas feels a powerful desire to kill the master of the dungeon and seize the amulet."

In that instant, Egam understood the meaning of the dark look in this man's—Iarumas's—eyes. To the man in black, Egam wasn't even an enemy—he was just an obstacle. Not even the end goal. Egam was something to be climbed over and then left behind. A hindrance, only there to be overcome.

And to do it, Iarumas wouldn't hesitate to die.

Egam was terrified. His fear escaped as a scream that echoed through the darkness.

"Are you insane?!"

No, Iarumas wouldn't hesitate to die. It was easy to put it into words like that. Especially here in this dungeon. However, death was meant to be terrifying. Pain. Suffering. No one could be indifferent to these things...

Besides, even though resurrection was available, it wasn't perfect. It was still possible Iarumas's soul would be lost. Complete death, not even allowing for reincarnation of the soul—the total loss of one's being from this world, this universe.

"And what do you plan to do if one comes up tails?"

Iarumas smiled.

"When that time comes, then the next adventurer will take care of it."

His bloodied left hand formed signs.

"Taila (*O swift wind*)!"

He had chanted this spell so many times.

"Tazanme woarif (*Together with the light*)!"

He couldn't possibly forget it.

"Iyeta (*Be unleashed*)!!!"

TILTOWAIT.

"Wha...?!"

Egam's eyes went wide. A seventh level spell... It was beyond imagining. This was the kind of stuff spoken of only in legends.

The flash obliterated Egam's zone with white darkness, and an intense heat assaulted him.

His scream went unheard. His pain unfelt. All that remained was the sensation of heat.

Eyes boiled. Skin blistered. He couldn't breathe. Yet Egam's mind was conscious of it all.

He grasped the amulet as if clinging to a lifeline. It was keeping him alive—as long as he had it, he wouldn't die.

The amulet was everything.

"Aghhh?!"

Suddenly, the arm clutching the amulet was chopped off.

Egam screamed. Not for the loss of his arm, but for the loss of the amulet.

What happened? Who? How?

Confusion and terror swam in Egam's muddy white eyes as they saw the last thing they ever would.

There. Hiding her tiny form in Iarumas's shadow and skillfully avoiding the scorching air…

She had located him in the darkness.

"Growl!!!"

Garbage hacked his head from his neck.

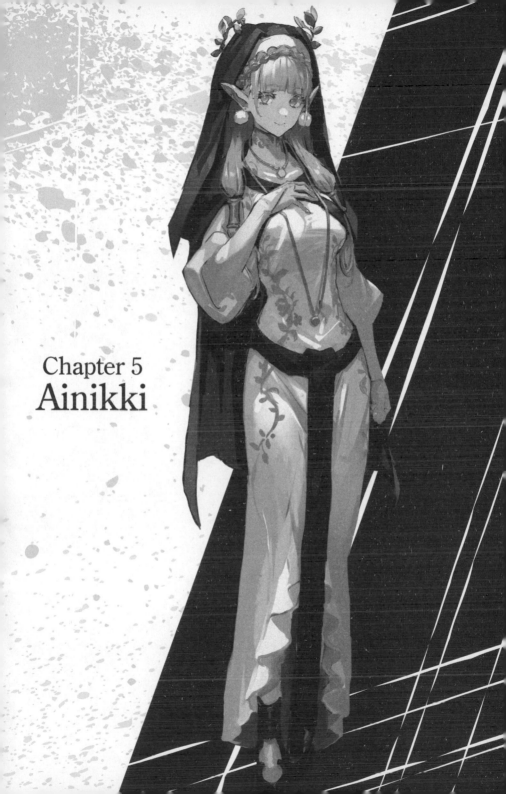

Chapter 5
Ainikki

"■■■■!!!"

Someone shouted a name. One that was awfully familiar.

He opened his eyes in the dark. But the scene that spread out before those eyes was also dark.

No.

An aberrant monster baring its fangs deep in the blackness of the dungeon. It had a huge body, dark blue with exposed muscles, and its eyes were fiery.

A greater demon.

Its arms, like great trees, thrust forward, unleashing a lethal storm of ice and freezing air.

It's MADALTO! That was what the man had meant to shout. His field of vision spun.

From that point on, scenes rushed by too fast to follow.

He saw enchanted equipment sparkling with a diamond-like magic—it floated into the air, attacking all on its own. Mages and fighters who called themselves examiners traded blows with shinobi, offering the man praise that seemed worse than foolish.

Inside a great, rocky cavern, he dodged the attacks of primordial monsters, wandering in search of treasure.

In each of these eras, he had been an adventurer. So, too, had the dungeon been there.

Burned, decapitated, petrified, level-drained—he'd died many times. And each time, even when he'd been turned to ash, he had returned from the underworld to challenge the dungeon once more.

Ultimately, he might've been no different from those risen dead.

The man laughed a little as that thought occurred to him. Not that he knew what he was laughing at.

In time, before he knew it, he found himself in a dusky burial chamber.

Not alone—with everyone. The chamber was filled with thick magical energy. Its source…the old man right before their eyes.

The old man's eyes glinted, flashing a bizarre light that burned with a mixture of madness and reason, neither sundered from the other. This mage, who was served even by the king of the undead, held something that shone with pale white brilliance.

The amulet.

He understood instinctively.

He needed to get his hands on it.

It was why the man was still here. The only reason.

"■ ■ ■ ■!!!"

Someone was calling his name. That awfully familiar name…

He answered his comrade's voice, lunging forward with his katana held tight. He closed in. Got within range.

The mad mage's mouth opened. He spoke words of true power.

O swift wind, be unleashed together with the light.

Wind. Light. Heat. White darkness consumed everything.

Snap! The man's consciousness cut out, sinking away once more.

He couldn't see anything now.

Couldn't hear.

All that remained was…

Murmur, prayer, chant, and then, command.

Pray.

§

"Iarumas!"

His eyes flew open.

He'd been hauled up onto land from the sea of slumber.

His mouth opened. He couldn't breathe. Oh, right. The air didn't suit him here. This was a different place.

Unable to bear it, he sat up. He couldn't inhale. Choking. His lungs weren't moving.

"Calm down. It's okay," a soft voice whispered in his ear. A cool, white hand stroked his back—Iarumas's back.

Surely, the death god's hand must be this gentle and beautiful.

"Yes, you're okay. You have been allowed to live. Calm down..."

Calm down. You're okay. These words which she repeated had less effect on him than the timbre of her voice.

Forcing a gasping breath through his hoarse throat, Iarumas filled his lungs with oxygen. Then, after a momentary pause, he rasped out, "Sister Ainikki."

"Yes," the silver-haired elf at Iarumas's side answered him with a smile. "Welcome back."

At that moment, Iarumas finally realized that he was on the altar of the temple. This, too, was familiar—something he had experienced many times.

Iarumas wondered what he ought to say. He opened his mouth, but no words came out. After some indecision, he murmured, "Thought I died..." as if it were the most inconsequential thing.

"You did," Aine said, exasperated. "And just who do you think prayed to God for KADORTO on your behalf?"

With a great sigh, Iarumas turned his eyes toward Sister Ainikki. The silver-haired elven lass had a look on her face like none he'd seen from her before.

What should he say? Iarumas was, uncharacteristically, a little unsure.

"So, you can make that kind of face too, huh?"

Aine was quiet for a moment. Then, she offered him a broad smile and said, "Even if we will meet again someday in the City of God, it's still sad, having to part for such a long time."

"I'm grateful," said Iarumas. "And I guess I should thank Sezmar too."

Aine let out a deep sigh. Without another word, she pointed her finger at Iarumas's knees. Following her gesture with his gaze, Iarumas finally realized one part of why his body had felt so heavy.

It wasn't just because he'd died, apparently.

A young girl had thrown her slender frame onto his lap with no regard for restraint, and she was now dozing away.

Iarumas reached out to Garbage's curly hair and awkwardly began combing it with his fingers. "Ahh," she murmured.

"Sezmar-sama came across the girl as she was dragging you back."

"And Raraja?"

"If you mean the thief boy, then he was with him too."

"I see…" In that case, Iarumas would have to thank Raraja too.

The man continued absentmindedly stroking Garbage's hair as he considered all of this.

"Umm…" Garbage sighed. Her unexpectedly long lashes fluttered as her eyelids twitched. Then her eyes snapped open, and she stared at Iarumas's face. "Arf!" she barked, puffing her chest up with pride.

She offered him something small—a fragment, no larger than a coin. With its shine lost, it was just an old piece of metal now…but there was no mistaking it.

It was the amulet that had hung from the mage's neck.

"You brought back more than just me, huh? This too?"

"Yap!"

"You sure worked hard…"

"Ahem!"

Iarumas took the amulet from Garbage, who looked so pleased with herself that he thought she might start wagging her tail.

But…

No.

This was only a shard of the amulet. A fragment, one of hundreds.

The mage had been able to wield all that power with only this much of it? Or…was even that massive magical accomplishment limited because he had so little?

This tiny shard was nothing compared to the object in Iarumas's memories. Even so…getting a fragment of the amulet was like a badge of honor for any adventurer.

Iarumas was staring vacantly at the shard, wondering what he ought to do with it, when…

"Back with the living again, are we?!"

The door slammed open. His attention turned to Sezmar.

The free knight, blond and masculine, had apparently made it back in one piece.

"You didn't die, then?" asked Iarumas.

"Unlike you," Sezmar retorted with a jovial laugh.

Raraja was beside him. It seemed like the boy didn't know what kind of expression he should be making at the moment. Had he matured somewhat after the fight underground? He looked at Iarumas, then pursed his lips and said, "Aw, man… You went and croaked on us in the end…"

"I'm an adventurer, after all," Iarumas said, nodding. "It comes with the territory."

"In that case, I'm gonna make it all the way down to the bottom without dying once."

"A good goal. I'll look forward to seeing it."

Iarumas wasn't being sarcastic, but Raraja snorted in response.

"You could have worded that better," Sezmar said, laughing.

Iarumas brushed him off with an, "Oh, yeah?" He didn't feel the need to rephrase. It wasn't that important. No, in Iarumas's mind, the important thing was—

"I believe I need to thank you somehow."

—settling the debt. Be it money, equipment, or some action. Everything came with a price attached.

Sezmar just smiled and shrugged. "Buy me a drink next time, would you?"

"Is that going to be enough?" Iarumas asked. Sezmar's request had been surprisingly humble. A high-level adventurer like him could afford to be greedier. Even if he was of good alignment.

The question made Sezmar's smile deepen. "Sarah and Moradin have been nagging me to tell them the story of how you died."

"I doubt it'll end with just that…" Knowing the two of them, they'd ask relentless questions and go digging into every possible detail. Iarumas crossed his arms, thinking that their scrutiny would be a rather high price to pay after all.

But then, Raraja's voice cut through his contemplation. "In that case," Raraja said, seeming to have found his resolve. "Find a body for me. You're a corpse hunter, aren't you?"

"Not really."

Raraja continued as if Iarumas hadn't responded. "It's a rhea girl. She's been dead a while now, though. Her body may be gone."

"Doubtful..." Iarumas shook his head slowly. It wasn't that he was feeling emotional about this. He had no interest in the girl Raraja wanted to search for. However, he spoke plainly, telling the boy the facts as he knew them. "If there's even a piece of her left, even a bone, then resurrecting her won't be impossible. It's worth trying, at least."

Before he could say he'd take on the task, Raraja leaned in and exclaimed, "Really?!"

Iarumas smiled a little. "If I lied to you about this, I'd have to be evil, wouldn't I?"

"They heard you say it! Sezmar, Garbage, and the sister too! They all heard you, okay?!"

"Yeah, I know."

Did the boy have a reason to be so over the moon about this? Iarumas didn't know. But even without knowing, he liked how this felt.

Ultimately, as far as adventures went, they'd struck out this time. Though they'd found an unexplored area of the dungeon, that was where the discoveries had ended. No treasure, and Iarumas had died, only to be resurrected again. Nothing gained.

And yet...

It doesn't feel so bad.

"I hate to bring this up when you're in such fine spirits, but..." A sharp voice addressed Iarumas, who was still on the altar. Sister Ainikki. She wore a beaming smile worthy of a saint. "Could I ask you to pay the tithe for your resurrection?"

"It wasn't paid already...?"

"We took everything you had on you, and it still wasn't enough, so we'll be adding the rest to your debt, okay?" Still smiling, Aine added, "You are a high-level adventurer, after all."

Iarumas gazed wordlessly up at the temple's ceiling, high and distant. He then looked beside him. For some reason, Garbage barked out an "Arf," with a look of pride on her face.

Since he was already in debt to Sezmar and Raraja, there was no point in turning to them for help.

In the end, Iarumas held up the shard of metal he was holding for Aine to see. "Can I pay you with this?"

"Just how many coins of the same size are you going to try to claim that little metal plate is worth?"

It wouldn't be a fair trade, she said. But…not fair for who, exactly?

Sezmar let out a deep sigh.

There's nothing else for it, Iarumas thought as he reached out and started vigorously mussing the curly hair of the girl on his lap.

"Aah?!" she protested, looking up at him resentfully.

He met her gaze. Her clear, blue eyes were like two bottomless lakes.

"You're coming with me to take responsibility for this."

Her response was a single bark.

"Ruff!"

§

It's not as though anything dramatically changed after that.

There was the same *clink, clink* as something small and metal bounced across the floor of the dungeon. With each step (space, area, whatever you want to call the measure) Iarumas moved, he threw his coin and reeled it back in.

The Creeping Coin always crawled back to him. He took another step and threw it again.

The same thing, over and over. There were no easy paths in the dungeon—not in any sense of those words.

"We've seriously gotta do this?"

But that didn't mean it wasn't discouraging.

Iarumas answered Raraja's grumbling as he reeled in the coin. "Not really, no."

"For real?!"

"Yeah."

Recently, Iarumas felt as if they were talking more during their explorations. Though, as far as he was concerned, that was about the only change.

"I'm no thief," said Iarumas, "but I hear that, with some experience, a thief can see through traps on the walls and floor."

"And until I've got that experience...?"

"We take it slow and steady."

"Urgh..." Despite his groaning, Raraja had a smile on his face.

It might be fair to say that their adventures had changed him.

Hmm.

Iarumas was amused to find himself thinking about that. When he recalled the past, he felt as though he'd seen his companions' growth as a positive thing back then too. Was this because of those vague memories he glimpsed? The visions he'd witnessed while hovering between life and death?

Yet even those dreams were as ephemeral as bubbles, sure to fade away upon waking...

"We'll have to start by teaching you to draw a map."

"A map?" asked Raraja. "Of the dungeon?"

"No one else is going to draw it for you, right?"

"Urgh..."

"Arf."

In a sense, all of this was thanks to the girl who had just emerged from a burial chamber covered in blood.

Finding Garbage had been a turning point for Iarumas.

That girl, who still had that crude iron collar around her neck, was dragging something heavy behind her.

A corpse.

It obviously belonged to an adventurer...but the body was so thoroughly destroyed that there was no identifying them. The best Iarumas could manage was to look at their boots—the style suggested that this corpse was probably a woman. Likely an elf or a human.

"Good work."

"Yap!"

When Iarumas mussed Garbage's hair with his gauntleted hand, she let out a bark. She tolerated it now, at least. Though, as for if she'd grown attached to him, he still doubted it.

Ultimately, nothing had changed...with one sole exception: these three were now exploring the dungeon together.

Iarumas idly pondered things as he pulled the body bags out of his pack. It was unusual for him. There wasn't anything he should be thinking about other than the dungeon.

Could it be, perhaps...? It was too much to say he'd changed, but maybe...something more subtle than that?

Yes. He was finding out that talking to others like this was...

Not that unpleasant.

It surprised Iarumas to discover this about himself, but he accepted it for what it was. How would Sister Ainikki react if he told her?

"Ow?!"

His thoughts were interrupted by a sudden cry—Garbage had apparently kicked Raraja hard in the shin.

"H-Hey, you! Cut that out, okay?!"

"Arf."

Raraja's objections did him no good. She gestured to the burial chamber with her chin, then trotted off in that direction.

Raraja followed behind her, holding his leg and whining. "If there's a chest, just say so... With words!"

They were just play-fighting—getting kicked wouldn't lower anybody's focus (HP). The boy would be able to open the treasure chest just fine.

But what if Raraja messed up somehow? If Garbage got caught up in something again?

Iarumas thought for a moment, then murmured to himself. It

was a word he'd long forgotten, one that was said when such things happened.

"Whoops..."

§

"Hey, look at that."

"Iarumas, huh..."

"Iarumas of the Black Rod..."

"He's a corpse looter."

"Damn that maggot..."

"I heard he recently got himself a slave girl."

"A disposable pawn? Poor thing."

"Who even knows how true his story is? What kind of man doesn't remember the things that happened in his past?"

"Oh, shut up! Make way, make way!" Raraja shouted, scattering the people in the crowd who were looking at Iarumas the same way they always did. As the onlookers shuffled away from him, eyes wide with surprise, he glared at them. "If you people die, I'm not hauling you back!"

It was afternoon in Scale.

Even if most of the people around were adventurers, shouting out loud on the street still drew attention. Raraja was fine with it.

Was his boldness because of the self-confidence he had begun to develop from his adventures? Perhaps it could also be seen as overconfidence... In which case, there *would* be people who got ideas.

The boy made money from corpse-hauling. Even had a slave girl with him. Adventurers would want to prey on them.

But even if people tried...

I'm backing him up, huh?

It didn't suit Iarumas at all.

He shook his head slowly, once more adjusting the position of the cord on his shoulder that he used to carry the body bag.

"There's no need to make a fuss," Iarumas said. "There'll be no end to it."

"Shut up." Raraja glared at the man. "It bugs me!"

"Well then, there's nothing I can do about that." If it was a problem with Raraja, then there was no helping it.

"Arf!" Garbage gave an energetic bark. Just how much did she understand?

No matter what path we take from here, it's sure to be a lively one. Just as Iarumas thought that...

"Woof..."

Garbage suddenly shrank into herself and backed away, seeming afraid.

This behavior—one she had hardly ever displayed in the dungeon— caused Iarumas to cock an eyebrow.

"Hey. What's wrong?" he asked. Obviously though, he would get no meaningful reply.

Raraja figured it out for him. "Ahhh." The boy smirked. "Her natural enemy's here."

"Garbage-chan!!!"

The elven priest was unbelievably quick. She raced in, light on her feet, and wrapped her slender arms around the even slighter frame of the girl.

"Yap?!"

Sarah ignored such cries and rubbed her cheek against Garbage. "Honestly, Iarumas! How could you make this girl haul corpses too?!"

"She's not carrying it."

"You're making her help, so it's the same! You hear me? The same!"

Garbage moaned pitifully, her eyes pleading Raraja to do something, anything, to save her. But Raraja wasn't going to oblige. He just smiled, his grudge over the earlier shin-kick written all over his face.

Well, let them do as they please. Iarumas smiled ever so slightly. He'd spotted five more acquaintances behind Sarah.

The All-Stars were each wearing their own unique but powerful equipment. They weren't tinged with the smell of blood, but they were fully equipped. That meant they were likely on their way into the dungeon.

Noticing Iarumas's "luggage," High Priest Tuck bowed his head slightly. Even if the dwarf had no idea who the remains belonged to, they deserved to be paid respect. Whether they were going to be resurrected or lost forever, death was still death…

"Have you heard, Iarumas?!"

But the free knight, Sezmar, ignored that fact, behaving like his usual, jovial self. He seemed ready to let out a raucous laugh at any moment, and without a doubt, there was a smile hidden inside his helm.

Sarah had run ahead of the group, but Sezmar strode on over now, and the rest of his party trailed behind him.

"Heard what?" Iarumas asked.

"About that corner of the third floor," Sezmar answered. "The monsters come back no matter how many times you kill 'em. I hear it's turned into a good place to make money."

"What strange tastes some people have."

"Aw, don't be like that! Everyone wants money and experience."

"I don't recall saying it was a bad thing."

"No, you didn't," Sezmar replied seriously before breaking into a laugh. "Well, do you know about *this*, then?"

"Again, what are you talking about?"

"The burial chamber. They're apparently calling it the Monster Allocation Center."

"Hmm…"

Allocation center. Iarumas liked the ring of it. It was a good name with a familiar sound.

But, if Iarumas were to change one thing about it…

"It's a shame it's not on the fourth floor."

"Sometimes, you say stuff that makes no sense."

Iarumas laughed. "Yeah, I don't get the stuff I say either."

They engaged in some more frivolous banter after that, then went their separate ways.

"Time to go!" Prospero shouted as he tore Sarah away from Garbage. The elven priest waved and said, "See you later!"

Finally free, Garbage gave a disgruntled "Woof!" and headed for Raraja. Iarumas ignored the sound of the thief boy shouting in pain from another hard kick to the shin, and he shouldered the corpse again.

The All-Stars would be going to the dungeon, while he—*they*—were going to the temple.

As Iarumas started walking his own way, he heard the sound of hurried footsteps behind him. Without having to look, he could tell that it was a boy and girl racing to catch up.

§

"Oh, Iarumas-sama! I see you worked hard again today."

When they reached the temple, Sister Ainikki was waiting for them with her usual smile. She saw the body bag Iarumas was hauling, and her smile loosened, growing even softer.

"I hope they were able to live and die well..." She made a holy sign in front of her chest. "Oh, my," she exclaimed, her eyes widening. "Raraja-sama and Garbage-sama are with you, I see. Why don't you all come inside? I'll put on tea."

"You mean it?" Raraja said exuberantly. There were a lot of people, not just Raraja, who would be overjoyed to have tea with Sister Ainikki.

In contrast to Raraja, who headed right in, Garbage stayed where she was, looking undecided.

"Hmmmmmm..." she groaned, then fell silent. She was on her guard. It was probably because of the bitter experience she'd had... The bath. However, her hesitancy soon faded, so she must have decided that it hadn't been as bad as dealing with Sarah. Or perhaps she thought that since Raraja was going, she'd have to as well.

"Yap." With that short bark, Garbage trotted after the thief.

That left just the two of them.

Murmurs, prayers, chanting.

Those sounds filled the quiet temple, ebbing and flowing like the tide.

"Come along. We'll have to deposit this person in the morgue..." Aine said, reaching out to accept the body bag from Iarumas. It seemed, surprisingly, that the strength she'd demonstrated the other day was of use in her normal duties as a woman of the cloth—hefting a corpse was certainly a workout.

"By the way," Iarumas said, finally picking up on something that had been nagging at him. "Who paid for my resurrection?"

"Hm?" Aine tilted her head to the side. A question mark seemed to hover over her. "I told you I'd be putting it on your tab, didn't—"

"*The first time*," he clarified.

Ohhh. Sister Aine smiled and answered, "It was me, you know?"

"I figured as much." There was no way she would have resurrected him by mistake.

The bashful sister and the stony-faced Iarumas. How would they have looked to anyone watching? Not that either of them would have cared.

"But...why?"

"Hm... It's nothing all that complicated." Aine's beautiful, slender fingers played with the hem of her habit. It was a gesture common for a girl of her age. Then, after some time, she let out a sad sigh. "I was a little... curious. For some reason..."

"Curious of what?"

"What were you born to do? And what did you die trying to accomplish?"

Iarumas didn't respond, and Sister Ainikki didn't press those questions further. Instead, she wanted to confirm one thing with Iarumas.

"Would you rather...I hadn't?"

"No," he answered. "I'm grateful you resurrected me."

"Well, I'm glad—"

Just as Sister Ainikki smiled, out of nowhere, a gust of wind blew through the temple. It played with her silver hair, making Aine narrow her eyes and hold down her wimple.

As she did, she noticed Iarumas's lips moving. They formed words she couldn't hear, even with elven ears, which despite her race's decline, were far more sensitive than a human's.

"Did you just say something...?"

"Nothing of importance." Iarumas laughed. "*Just you wait.*"

§

In ancient times, long ago, the people forgot it.

Who can say how many years passed after that? One day, when no one knew it had ever existed, it abruptly returned.

The dungeon.

This magical hole, suddenly gouged out of the land, was literally overflowing with power. It plunged deep into the ground—no one knew how far—and was filled to the brim with monsters and treasure.

Naturally, many self-proclaimed heroes, saints, and sages braved its depths one after another. Many of the evil villains who roam our world also attempted to seize the dungeon for themselves. All of them were swallowed up by it, destroyed.

A descendant of the legendary hero. A great sage who spent their life in the study of magic. A brash youngster from the village.

Inside the dungeon, they were all equal—the weakest of the weak.

No one knew what the dungeon was. They only knew two things, and perhaps, just one.

Treasures lay sleeping within, ones that transcended the imagination. The dungeon was also home to man-eating monsters and filled with lethal traps.

In short, all anyone knew was that the dungeon was a place beyond the comprehension of mankind—a completely different world.

People came to view the dungeon as dangerous, so they kept a respectful distance from it. But the products that came from the dungeon were—in a variety of ways, and to a variety of people—still alluring. There was no shortage of people who ventured into the dungeon seeking wealth and fame, to do deeds of arms, or for some other purpose.

Dying repeatedly, overcoming danger, and seizing treasure—some gradually adapted to the dungeon.

In time, people came to call them...adventurers.

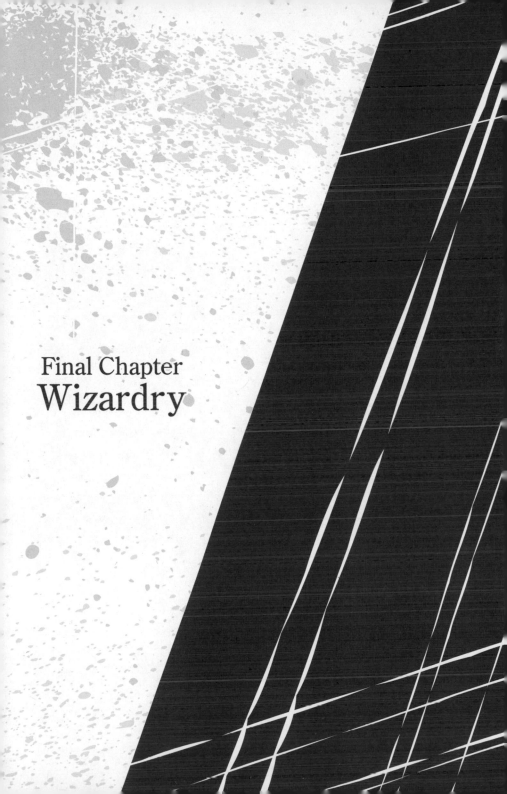

Final Chapter
Wizardry

In the depths of darkness, deep beneath the earth...

From the midst of slumber, her eyelids rose slightly.

She felt as though that familiar breeze, laden with the scent of ashes, had reached him.

This was a horrible place filled with all this world's calamities, where miasma that rose from the demon hole swirled.

No wind could blow here. The air was stagnant, clouded, rotten. And yet...

Could it be...that one?

There was no proof. Yet, for some reason, she felt it was. Truly, it amused her.

Suddenly, a voice spoke. "It would seem that way, ancient one."

The one who appeared from the darkness was... Ah, yes, her old friend. Just as she'd expected.

The great old wizard who served as one of the four gatekeepers.

She made the air shake in response. A laugh, perhaps?

"Hawkwind brought word, you see..."

In that case, the girl was likely fine. The gatekeeper nodded gravely, confirming what she already suspected.

"The girl is fine. Fine, indeed, ancient one. The bloodline of Alavik and Margda has been protected..."

Then there is nothing to worry about.

That one was at the bloodline's side. Everything was proceeding smoothly.

However, the gatekeeper looked unhappy. The great old wizard shook his head as if lamenting all the misfortunes of this world.

"But *he* is immature… He's been weakened greatly, perhaps by the forceful resurrection."

Of course he is. Did we not know that all along?

It had happened long ago… When the demon hole first opened— when the light of the divine instrument dimmed—when the blessing of the Goddess was lost.

Those who had been reincarnated and sent in…had lost much of their power. They'd known all about it.

"There will be many troubles. It *might* be possible. However…it may also prove impossible…" The gatekeeper wore a look of exhaustion, just as he had the time when he'd been sealed in the cosmic cube.

"O friend, they may not reach us before the seal is broken…"

They should be able to, she responded to the gatekeeper. *It was that way once. And so it will be this time too…because every adventurer has been that way. Shouldn't you know this better than anyone?*

"Oh, I see…" The gatekeeper's wrinkled face smiled. "I suppose you're right."

Indeed, I am, she said, then addressed the gatekeeper by his old name.

"The flow of time is cruel, ancient one," the gatekeeper said. He then departed, disappearing as he had appeared.

She understood what her friend was saying. There were none now remaining who knew their names.

Those nostalgic days, when youth went hand-in-hand with ashes, were long in the past. It was unclear what meaning there was in continuing to wait here. But truly, what point was there in worrying about that? In due time, someone would reach the bottom of the dungeon, and then all would be revealed.

And, without fail, someone would arrive in the depths of the demon hole to smash the calamity.

It mattered little whether *that one* would be the person to do it.

As long as there were still adventurers…

Believing this, the great dragon L'kbreth closed her eyes and went back to sleep.

The darkness descended once more.

Afterword

Hello, this is Kumo Kagyu.

If you're new to me, then nice to meet you, and if you're a returning reader, then good to see you again. But, um, what do I say? Oh, right! Wizardry! What a surprise, huh? I never imagined I'd be getting involved with this series.

Am I dreaming? Is it about time for me to wake up in bed...?

Speaking of the original Wizardry—the famous initial trilogy was last ported to the GBC and Wonderswan around the year 2000. That was more than two decades ago. I suspect that means many younger readers don't know Wizardry.

As awkward as I feel being the one to tell you about it, please, allow me to explain.

Once upon a time, two young men were obsessed with D&D, the world's first RPG. Now, this wasn't the kind of game you play on your game console. It was a game played with pens, paper, and dice.

This was the dawn of the personal computer era when PCs meant for individuals first began to appear. These two young men had a thought: what if they left all the bothersome RPG calculations and judgments to a computer? Yes, the story would be something so simple that *even a computer* could understand it.

A great wizard steals the source of a mad king's power, then flees deep inside a dungeon. Drifters with unclear origins—adventurers— gather to slay the great wizard. The dungeon awaits them, filled with dangerous traps and many monsters, as well as treasure and magic weapons. Even if adventurers fall along the way, they can be carried to the temple and resurrected...for an exorbitant tithe.

Life is cheap. Adventuring goes hand-in-hand with death. There is much humor to be found, and also, much danger.

Rabbits and ninjas appear alongside dragons to decapitate people in this bizarre world. But the adventurers fight back with their own weapons—the Muramasa and a blade inspired by a food mixer—then blast the enemy with nuclear explosions.

Thus, *Wizardry: Proving Grounds of the Mad Overlord* was born.

It was followed by several other titles. *The Knight of Diamonds*, where you explore a demonic hole in search of a lost suit of legendary armor and a holy staff; *Legacy of Llylgamyn*, where you travel to a sacred dragon atop a holy mountain in order to uncover the cause of recent disasters; *Return of Werdna*, which depicts the return of the great wizard who was supposedly slain.

WIZ was brought to Japan, ported to the Famicom, and became a novel, manga, anime, and TRPG. There was *Tonariawase no Hai to Seishun, Llylgamyn Bouken Kitan*…and even a 4-koma manga. They even made Japan-exclusive spin-off games, and we got our hands on the rights.

For some reason, Japanese people love this strange, brutal, and humorous world. Its influence is found in many works—anime, manga, games, movies, light novels…

I myself was one of the people influenced by this franchise, and I've written works that show signs of that influence. Even so, I was only properly introduced to WIZ back around the time when it got its last port. In truth, I was simply following in the footsteps of those adventurers who came before me, amazed at what I saw.

And yet…look at me now.

Before I knew it, I was in a position to be writing a Wizardry novel. Seriously, I'm not about to wake up in bed soon, right…?

This book is my interpretation of what Wizardry might be like. I can't boastfully say, "This is WIZ!" and there may be people who feel I've gotten it wrong. But, please, smile and nod at those inevitable shortcomings. In my eyes, your adventurers seemed so cool, so interesting.

If anyone is encountering WIZ for the first time through this work, please, go back and play the games. There you will find the story of *your* adventure—one that's only for you to know. And I would be glad if all of you, whether you go in knowing WIZ or not, could enjoy this work.

Thankfully, it seems that they're going to let me write another volume. Iarumas, Garbage, and Raraja's next adventure will start after they've gotten some rest at the inn. If you would come along with them, nothing would make me happier.

Until we meet again.